THE FUGITIVES

BORGO PRESS BOOKS BY ARDATH MAYHAR

THE FUGITIVES

A Tale of Prehistoric Times

by

Ardath Mayhar

The Borgo Press
An Imprint of Wildside Press

MMVIII

CONTENTS

ABOUT THE AUTHOR

The author of sixty-two books, more than forty of them published commercially, **ARDATH MAYHAR** began her career in the early eighties with science fiction novels from Doubleday and TSR. Atheneum published several of her young adult and children's novels. Changing focus, she wrote westerns (as **Frank Cannon**) and mountain man novels (as **John Killdeer**), four prehistoric Indian books under her own name, and historical western *High Mountain Winter* under the byline **Frances Hurst**.

Recently she has been working with on-line publishers. *A Road of Stars* was her first original novel to appear in print-on-demand format. Many of her out-of-print titles are now available from e-publishers fictionwise.com and renebooks.com; many other novels are being published by the Borgo Press Imprint of Wildside Press and Amazon.com.

Now in her seventies, Mayhar was widowed in 1999, after forty-one years of marriage, and has four grown sons. She now works at home, writing short fiction and nonfiction, and doing book doctoring professionally. Her web pages can be found at:

w2.netdot.com/ardathm/ and
http://ofearna.us/ books/mayhar.html

FOREWORD

We live in a very safe and easy time, in the history of our world. But there was, many thousands of years in the past, no safety and little ease for the tribes of human beings living in Europe and Asia and Africa.

On the average, a person was old at thirty, if he lived that long, and seldom did anyone live to see the age of sixty. At twelve or fourteen, a young person was considered an adult, ready for the responsibility of marriage and parenthood.

Now we choose what we want to do with our lives. It may be a good thing to look back, from time to time, at an era when only the rules of the tribe safeguarded its people and directed their lives. Those who defied those rules must leave the security of the place and people they knew, going away into a forest without end, among animals that were huge and fierce and hungry.

As well, those early religions could be very grim, whether conducted by shamans or Grand-mothers or Holy Ones. Death was usually the penalty for breaking the laws. This is the story of a pair of youngsters who were forced by circumstances to defy the laws of their tribes and the rules of their religions.

One can only speculate about the distant past, for no records exist from those times except fossils and spear-points and cave drawings. Yet we do know something, and observing primitive peoples who exist now, in our own time, can tell us more.

Here, then, is the story of Bain and Arma, who broke the law because they were caring human beings.

—Ardath Mayhar
Chireno, Texas

CHAPTER ONE

THE HUNTER

 ☼DEFIANCE☼

The boy ran blindly through the forest, his eyes dimmed with unshed tears. The deer hide cloak he wore had worked loose from its ties at his belt, as he fled through the dim aisles of trees, and was flapping at his legs and catching, from time to time, on bushes along the path.

He tugged it free without pausing. Only his hunter's long training kept him from making enough noise to attract one of the prowling predators that stalked the night-bound game-trails.

He paused at last, even his hard muscles and strong lungs needing rest. Leaning against a tremendous oak, he scrubbed at his eyes with grimy fingers, wiping away the tears. His heart still pounded, and he breathed through his mouth, easing the air in and out as silently as he could. He could not know what pursuers might now be on his trail, intent upon his punishment and his death.

He strained his ears, but the drumming of his

pulse drowned out everything but the song of his blood and the thudding in his chest. If the shaman had sent the best of the tribe's hunters after him, they would come quickly. He could not rest for long.

The moon hung full in the east, caught among the branches of another oak. Thin shards of light trickled through the thick-leaved branches as the full moon of late summer lit the forest. That marked the sacrifice to the hunters' god, every seventh year.

Seven summers—half of Bain's life—had passed since the last offering of the blood of the best hunter in the tribe, who went to the god to assure his fellows of good hunting for another span of seasons. Bain hardly remembered the flames of the torches, the red-gold of the moon, or the still shape of the man tied to the Holy Tree. He had been very young, then.

Bain shivered and forced himself upright. This year the sacrifice was his own father, who was perhaps the finest hunter the tribe had ever produced. Balit had taught his son all he knew, and this year the Shaman had ordained that Bain must complete the sacrifice, kill his father, and then step into his father's place as first hunter of the People.

Now tears spilled down his cheeks. He had known from the first that he could not tighten the leather cord, strangling his father slowly, as the ritual prescribed. Normally his training would have been given by his mother's brother, but he was one of the unfortunates who had no living uncle. His father taught him, because of that, and they had become very close.

Although it went against all his training and the

beliefs of his people, Bain had no wish to be tied to that tree, in another seven years, and strangled by a new hunter. It was not a good thing to think about. Death came, yes, but, if you were fortunate, not before you were older, had reared children, and were of no more use to the tribe.

The moon was now high above the thick mat of overhanging trees. His father was dead by now, he knew, no matter how furious the Shaman might be at having his commands defied. Another had sent him into the realm of the god, but it had not been the hand of his son, and the boy was grateful for that.

Bain was, whatever he might think or feel now, an outcast. He had lost any right even to the air he breathed, here on the tribal hunting ground. If he were caught—he pushed the thought away. Death was nothing.

But the death the Shaman would devise for him, if those sent to hunt him should catch him, would be a terrible one; he did not intend to suffer it. He could almost see the ancient's toothless grimace as his wrinkled brown face presided over the sacrifice.

He realized with sudden surprise that he had hated the man since he was a child. He had a feeling the Shaman had also disliked and despised him, for he had never felt any respect for the powerful one. Only desperate fear of the wicked gleam in his cruel old eyes.

Thinking of him, he took up his flight again, his bare brown feet silent amid the leaves under the huge trees. His people knew this forest world from end to end of their chosen hunting territory. He must leave such familiar country if he would escape from that evil old man.

To the north there was the Cold Water, cutting off any flight. To the east there were rugged mountains, which he had no wish to tackle alone. But to the south there were people. Word about those barbarians had passed through the forest with the occasional lost hunter from another tribe.

The elders had debated whether these might be real human beings or perhaps demons who imitated their shapes, but word had come that they were men. If there were real people in the south, perhaps there might be space for one who tracked silently, killed cleanly, and could provide meat for a hungry clan.

There would be no help from his own people, not even his mother or his sisters. Yet as he left his mother's house he had found his leather cloak, rolled about his flint knife and his father's spear. His mother had done for him what she could, once his fate was decreed. Anything more would sentence her, too, to death.

Now he knew he must move through the moon-struck forest as far and as fast as he could. It was much better to die in the teeth of a giant bear or a huge cat than in any way the Shaman might invent.

* * * * * * *

He followed a game trail that ran southward, keeping the occasional glint of the moon on his left until it rose to the middle of the sky. The rolling shape of the land changed, as he ran, becoming steeper and rougher. Some time after the moon moved down in the west to hide behind the dense forest, he came out into a small clearing and found himself staring at the top of a bald knoll.

He blinked hard, his heart almost pausing in its steady pounding. A horned shape stood on that hilltop, its rack of antlers silhouetted against the disk of the moon. A huge stag was looking directly at Bain.

The Horned God himself! He had followed his disobedient servant to punish him, there was no doubt of that. Bain dropped to his knees and laid his forehead against the warm summer turf, now damp with dew.

Through the earth, he could feel the vibration of approaching hooves. He flattened himself against the ground, his tears flowing again. He cupped his head in both hands, waiting to die. The Shaman had taught him the Horned One allowed no disobedience and would punish those his priest sentenced.

The hoofbeats pattered nearer, muffled as they crossed thick grass, and became sharper as they climbed onto the rocky ridge where he lay. When they stopped, he thought the great beast must stand directly over him. He could smell the sharp wild scent of the stag, tanging the cool night air.

He waited for the thrust of those antlers, the hot rush of blood, the pain. Nothing happened, and at last he twisted his neck so he might look up.

Strong, slender legs stood beside him. Not man-legs, though the Shaman said the Horned God was half man. Yet that waiting shape was so calm and majestic Bain could not believe it to be anyone but the god himself.

The eyes, shining faintly in the moonlight, stared down, the delicate head cocked so the moonlight shimmered on the many points of that magnificent rack of horns.

Bain felt a surge of hope. This was not what the

Shaman had taught. Something was different...he rolled over and got to his feet, compelled by a will not his own. The god was commanding him, he thought.

When he stood upright beside the stag, his head came well below that of the god. The great beast snorted, casting at the same time a piercing glance at the boy. Then it turned its gaze toward the south and snorted again.

With alarming suddenness, it wheeled and bounded away across the clearing, up the knoll against the round moon, and out of sight. Bain stared after it, still seeing its moon-silvered shape behind his eyes.

So that was how it felt to stand face-to-face with a god! He had never known anyone, even the Shaman, who claimed to have done such a thing.

But now he knew his direction had been well chosen. The god had given him some sort of approval, he was certain. He had not trampled this escaped devotee into the dirt, bloody and gored to the bone. The god, instead, had looked at him gently and nodded toward the south.

Was the Shaman mistaken in the nature of the Horned God? Or...he shivered at the blasphemy of his thought...did he lie in order to hold power over the people?

With that puzzle in his mind, he set out again, southward, beneath the dark trees that closed about him as soon as he left the clearing.

CHAPTER TWO

THE JOURNEY

☼BAIN☼

When Bain paused at last to sleep, the moon had been down for some time and dawn light was in the summer sky. He climbed into a tree, hooking his strong toes into crannies in the bark or about convenient branches, until he found a crooked branch large enough to hold his body securely. It was not the most comfortable sleeping place, but he had no intention of waking in the teeth of a bear or a wolf.

He woke, stiff and a bit chilled, after a few hours of deep sleep. Wide awake instantly, as a hunter must be, he was ready to go forward at once, for any pursuit the Shaman might send would be moving fast on his track.

As he rubbed the sleep from his eyes, the birds, who had been singing their late-summer calls through the trees, went silent. The stillness warned him to stay put, quiet as the squirrel on the next branch. Something moved through the trees, its heavy tread crackling leaves and twigs with the carelessness that only a large predator could afford.

Bain stretched along the branch on which he had slept, risking an eye over its curve to watch the path below. The steps came on without caution. Not a wolf—those were not a wolf's footfalls. It had to be a bear.

Bain had hunted with parties that detoured for miles to avoid those huge creatures. He had seen them, of course, from the safety of a tree and in the company of some lamed hunters who lacked arms or hands or parts of their faces. The missing parts had usually been left in the jaws of one of the great beasts, and those who left them counted themselves lucky. When a hunter did not return from the forest at all, most agreed that a bear had caught him.

The animal coming into sight below was frightening, even from a treetop. It stood half again as tall as a man, when it rose onto its hind legs to scent the air. Its claws were longer, he could tell when it stretched its arms aloft, than a man's fingers, as they glinted in the morning light.

It opened its mouth wide, yawning, and the teeth shone, too, their length and sharpness making Bain shudder. He had never seen the great bear from so near, and he knew his thin body would make only a snack for such a huge creature.

The bear's head turned, as if Bain's thought had brought him to its attention. The small black eyes scanned the trees until it found the shape of the boy high above. Even flattened to the branch, Bain knew he had been located, for the bear ambled over to snuffle the bark of the oak.

It rose onto its hind legs again, reaching as high as it could on the great trunk. The claws rasped as the creature raked strips of bark down the tree trunk.

Bain lay still, his nerves tingling with terror. The bear rumbled and groaned as it moved around the tree, stopping now and again to mark the bark once more. If it had been smaller and younger, it might have tried to climb after him, the boy knew, but luckily it was too heavy to work its bulk straight up that great trunk.

The sun was well up, its golden color staining the sky. Bain watched with despair, knowing hunters were speeding after him, all the while he was trapped in this tree. But he could do nothing but wait.

It seemed forever before the bear grew bored with staring up at its unreachable prey and crunched away down the trail, stopping to examine bushes for berries or to turn over logs after succulent grubs. Bain was almost beside himself before the thing was out of sight at last.

When it was gone, and he could no longer hear its progress, Bain climbed down on shaking legs, as much from lack of food as from fear, he assured himself. He went to one of the logs the bear had turned and sifted through the rotted wood with his fingers. A breakfast of grubs was far better than nothing at all.

When he rose, his stomach no longer growled, though he had to keep picking slivers of spongy wood from between his teeth. He had removed his deer hide cloak to cover him in the night, and now he rolled it and tied it behind his shoulder. Then he belted up his kilt, also made of deer hide, and began to run again.

The delay caused by the bear had also supplied

him with food. It was, he thought, a good trade, for now he had more energy.

He did not, of course, run carelessly through the forest. From time to time he was forced to climb or to hide when he located wild pigs or some of the smaller predatory cats. But he made good time, and by nightfall the forest was definitely thinner, the trees smaller than those he knew.

When he stopped to sleep, he had a hard time finding a tree tall enough to make a secure resting place. Wolves hunted at night, and demons and spirits moved in the darkness, all his people knew, threatening anyone who did not take precautions. A high perch was not much, but it was better than risking sleep on the ground.

Dawn found him ready to move, though this time he had to locate his own breakfast. Grubs from a fallen tree and berries from a bush helped him a bit, but he had begun craving meat. Yet there was no time to hunt. He had to get beyond the range of those who hunted him as quickly as possible.

Luck was with him, however, for he surprised a small hare in a burn-meadow and killed it with a stone from his sling. He walked steadily now, chewing the raw meat and feeling it provide new strength to his limbs. He ate part of the animal and saved the rest in his roll for later use.

He knew he would not be so lucky every time he needed food, and yet his journey, so far, had been supplied so easily it made him wonder. Was the god helping him on his way? After all, the Horned One was the god of hunters.

Although he had heard the hunters' tales, he had not really believed the world extended so very far.

He had heard descriptions, handed down through the years from the old tales, of trees and animals and lands and people that were not like those he knew, but now he was actually seeing such strange things. He found he had believed, somewhere deep inside, that the world ended beyond the familiar forests his people hunted.

He was entering a strange world, all alone, his people far behind. He could never return to his home, he knew, and lone hunters did not live long in the unforgiving forest. He remembered the Shaman driving out three young men who disobeyed him. Their well-gnawed bones had been found in the forest, many months later. The memory made him shiver.

Day followed day, and sometimes Bain grew so weary he forgot why he was traveling. He forgot he could never return to his home, and he almost turned back along his trail toward the familiar forest of the north and the cook fire before his mother's house.

But he always remembered in time and moved south again. Summer's last hot breath lay over the trees, whose growth was now thinner and the trees much smaller than those providing his sleeping places in lands now left behind. He found it harder to rest securely, and there came a night when he was hard put to find a suitable tree at all.

At last he found a grove of oaks, scrubby and short but well above the reach of most animals, and went up one like a squirrel, taking refuge in its top. Night sounds subtly different from those he knew in the north creaked and chirped and called about him. Yet he slept, exhausted with running, until light filled the sky again.

He found that from his perch he could look out across a long stretch of land holding no trees at all. He had never dreamed of a place without forest, and he stared in astonishment across the grassy waste. Then he used his hunter's training to orient himself.

As he surveyed the area, he found that an arm of forest looped out toward the grassland just south of his location. From beyond it rose a column of smoke, which brought him to instant alertness.

Forest fires were the terror of his people, for lightning storms often set them off in summer. His people had fled before the bellowing flames more than once, in his lifetime. Yet this was no line of smoke, as such a fire caused. It was a straight column, like one caused by a village's cook fires.

His belly was rumbling as Bain came down his tree, but it would have to wait. He could not take the time to hunt grubs until he saw for himself who had built that fire.

He moved silently through the wood. Working a fire-drill required patience and skill. The fingers grew numb with spinning the drill and grasping the bow. Igniting the tinder was a thing that could take much of a day, and when his mother taught him how to make fire he had given up many times before he found a spark he could bring to life in the shredded bark of the tinder.

Fire made life tolerable for his kind, and a people who held that secret might well be a tribe he could join. As he thought about this, he came to a spot in the scanty trees where there was a circle of ashes...a campfire.

The ashes were fresh and the dirt scattered over

them was still warm.

And then he heard a clear call ring through the air. Words were audible in that cry, but they meant nothing to him. He scrambled up the biggest tree he could find and hid among the leaves.

An animal loped up the game trail he had been following. A wolf? No, it was too small and not the right color. Its coat was patched with gray and brown and white. It wandered back and forth on either side of the path, nosing into patches of vine and bramble and barking, to his amusement, at butterflies and squirrels and hares.

Behind it came a woman. A girl, he corrected himself, though if he had not heard from hunters that other kinds of people existed he might have wondered what she was, for she looked very different. Though she was shaped roughly like his own kind, instead of being tall and slender and blond, she was short and square. Her hair was dark, and her skin was tanned to the shade of deer hide.

He was consumed with curiosity, but he did not relax his caution. The world was a dangerous place, and men feared each other with good reason. Wolves and bears and other predators just as fierce were not the only perils. Men often hunted men, those lost hunters had told his people, just as the beasts did.

Just as his own people now hunted him! He felt sudden shame at the thought.

The girl was sturdily built and looked friendly enough as she came up the path following the wolf-creature. Though she did not look like the girls in his own tribe, she did not seem at all frightening, though it was possible her people might be more dangerous than she looked.

She passed under his tree and went deeper into the thin forest. After a time she returned, and once she was out of sight he slid from the tree and went into the trees to hunt for his breakfast.

He was excited and filled with wonder. But he knew he must think out his approach carefully, for only by taking great pains did a hunter survive.

CHAPTER THREE

THE FARMERS

 **ARMA**

The Grandmother of her people had decided, two generations before, that the tribe must move up from the warm coastal plains where they had lived for so many generations. Arma wondered what their life had been like, there, for her mother had not been born when the move was made.

She also wondered why the Grandmother, the Mother, and the Daughter, elders and rulers of the tribe, had decided that such a change of location must be made. The weather, perhaps, had been one element in that decision. Or perhaps strangers had come, robbing the fields and the storehouses of her people.

She had spent much of her childhood bending over the garden plots, pulling out weeds or planting sprouts and seeds. She knew what a terrible loss it would be to have a crop stolen or burned, as it was rumored some barbaric tribes did. Here there were no intruders, though from time to time the watchers

had caught glimpses of tall, pale hunters in the forest north of the farmlands.

Now she was freed of the labor in the fields, for
she was apprenticed to Kalva, the herb woman, and
studied with her the effects of herbs and plants on
the sicknesses of their people. It was useful work,
and very interesting; now, in her twelfth summer,
she was becoming expert in such matters.

Even after so long, many of the things that grew
in this new land were still being tested, slowly and
cautiously, for their effects upon people and animals. She and Kalva gathered them, steeped them
into teas or boiled them for food or smashed them
into poultices and used them with great care. Tiny
amounts were given, and then the results were as-
sessed.

Kalva had lost only two apprentices in all the
time she had worked in this new country. Arma was
lucky to have been chosen to replace the last one,
and so far, in her year as helper to the herb woman,
nothing had done so much as make her sick to her
stomach.

On this bright, hot morning she was going after
more roots from the forest. With Roff, her family's
dog, she made for the thickest growth of trees. The
pair of them wandered about, checking into patches
of wild plants and taking strips of bark from trees,
leaves from shrubs, and roots that she dug from beneath patches of blossoming plants. In damp spots
she dug cat-tail roots and those of iris, as well.

As she cut and dug and picked and peeled, Arma
memorized the entire process. She pinned down the
location of the plant, the odor, texture, and taste,
touching her tongue very lightly to any cut surface.

All were fixed in her memory, and any useful substance could be found again without delay. Indeed, everything her people knew was stored in human minds, for they had no other way of recording vital information.

Working her way through the wood, she became aware that Roff was watching something in a treetop. She also felt eyes gazing at her, though she saw nothing there. Roff was valuable for many reasons, but most important was his function as a watchdog. She had been warned often of danger in the wood, because of his sharp bark and stiffening tail and ears.

She knew he hadn't decided if the thing he watched, whatever it might be, was dangerous. But when she bent over her digging stick, her back prickled.

She peeped from the corners of her eyes as she moved about, and at last she caught a glimpse of something bright in a tree. Golden hair caught a sunbeam, giving away the hiding place of the boy among the leaves.

She felt her heart thump with excitement. She had seen traders, up from the old home on the coast, with brown hair and black hair and ruddy braids. Tall, broad men in furs used to come, the old tales said, to trade with the people along the seacoast. In her own place, she had seen men who were very different from her own people.

Here, so far from the sea, where had this pale-haired person in the tree come from? She knew she should run back to the village and warn the men, who would come and catch this stranger, for legitimate traders came openly and in numbers. But the boy made no threatening move, and from his stillness she thought he might be frightened of her and of Roff.

Eyes and ears alert, she watched Roff. If this were only one of many, she would know in time to give warning, for the dog would never miss the presence of strange men. His eyes bright and his ears pricked up with interest, the dog ruffled his whiskers, wanting to bark but not, as yet, finding a reason to.

Covertly, as she moved about with her digging stick, Arma examined the newcomer. He looked thin and pale through the leaves, she thought, as if he had not eaten well in a very long while.

She moved out of range and dug some more, but as she worked she thought hard. The Grandmother had told the tribe about the light-skinned raiders who attacked the old villages. They caught goats and even women and carried them away into the unknown country that had spawned them. She had warned that there might be wild tribes in this new land who did not know the Mother Goddess and obey her laws.

But as long as Roff was not disturbed, Arma felt no fear. She felt certain the starved boy in the tree posed no problem for her.

Still, she was in duty bound to report his presence to the Mothers of the tribe, for they held the responsibility for the safety of all the families. They must know when anything unusual happened.

She felt reluctant to make that report, for she knew what the Grandmother's reaction would be. The old woman trusted nothing new or different.

It seemed to be her desire to keep everything

and everyone the same, obedient to herself and her daughter and granddaughter, unable to alter anything in their lives. Indeed, Arma knew the Grandmother feared nothing in the world more than losing her tight grasp on the life of the village. Kalva had said as much, though she did not know her apprentice could hear her words.

Once her bag was filled, Arma turned toward the village. As she moved out of the arm of woods, she saw ahead of her the three long, earth-covered houses that sheltered ten double-handfuls of her people by night.

Now most of those people were in the fields, harvesting the grain that had been bred over the years from grass with large seed-heads. Many tended the gardens of squash and beans and root vegetables, harvesting the crop, which would be dried in the sun to feed the people over the winter. This was good land, rich and productive. They would eat well all winter, even if the weather became harsher than it had been, so far.

Children with long sticks stood guard over the fields, driving out the wild birds that ate the grain or pecked the vegetables. Some of those youngsters brought down birds with stones, and later they would be added to pots of stew or spitted over the cook fires. She had spent her own time at that task, when she was small, and she smiled at her own small brother as she passed him.

Kalva lived alone in her cramped hut. Arma entered it after calling softly to warn the old woman of her arrival. The duties of an herb woman required quiet and solitude not to be found in the longhouse, amid fretting babies and women talking shrilly over the babble.

Her house was built of logs and bark and covered over with turf. She kept in it her herbs for medicines, and in front of it burned the fire needed for heating stones to boil water in her big earthen pots.

Arma slept outside, on the occasions when she might be needed, but usually she joined her family in the longhouse. She had wondered, of late, whether it might not be better to move into a shed of some sort attached to Kalva's hut, for there was more and more pressure from her parents and the Grandmother to submit to their will and marry. She did not want that.

Arma would be, in time, a fine herb woman, Kalva assured her. And for that she would need the solitude the old woman commanded. A husband and children would drive out her opportunity for learning her skills and finding her own place within the tribe as Healer, when the time came.

As she bent to enter the low doorway, she found herself feeling rebellious at the thought. What gave the Grandmother the right to rule over her life?

CHAPTER FOUR

THE BIRD CLAN

☼KALVA☼

As usual, Arma found the herb woman busy—this time she was pounding a sharp-smelling mess of leaves in her stone mortar, adding water from a jar from time to time. When Arma entered, she looked up and grunted.

"Did you find the sweet roots the children like to chew?" she asked. The rhythm of her hands did not alter.

"I dug a clump in the wood, enough for some to plant in the gardens, as well. I think that would be a good thing to grow, for it keeps the babies quiet."

Kalva nodded, her dark eyes twinkling in the dim light of the house. "They are good for that, and harmless. Sometimes it is a good thing to keep the infants still, and even those who whine the most will hush for a bit of root. In winter it will be wonderful, for some of the older people hate the noise."

She set aside the paste of leaves and began sorting through the things in Arma's bag. "It will be better when we build another longhouse, giving more room in each for the families. Until then, this will ease the cold season for those who want a bit of peace."

Arma was laying out a long rank of plants on the table of split logs that ran along one side of the small room. She sorted them as to variety and use, and as she worked she told Kalva where each had been found. The old woman would not forget one word of her tale, she knew.

Once she was finished, she knelt beside her teacher and looked up. "There is a boy in the forest," she said. "He is tall and pale, and his hair is the color of the sun. Roff spotted him in the top of a tree, so I pretended not to see, as he was hiding. I think he was afraid of us."

The herb woman stared down, her eyes wide. "Only one?" Her voice was sharp. "No others were with him there in the forest?"

Arma shook her head. "Roff would have known. He would have growled in that certain way and moved back toward the village, if there had been more than one stranger among the trees."

Kalva relaxed a bit. "True. Dogs are useful for such work. But where one stranger comes, others usually appear, sooner or later. I must take word of this to the Mothers."

Arma felt the weight of those words in the pit of her stomach. Something inside quailed at the thought of putting the skinny boy into the hands of the Grandmother.

As if she knew what her apprentice was feeling, Kalva shook her head. "We must not keep secrets from those who are responsible for our safety. I will go at once to the Grandmother, and she will tell the others. The men will hunt for this boy, and then we will see." She shooed Arma out of the hut ahead of her, as she wiped her hands on her goat-wool skirt.

Arma felt helpless, watching the old woman move through the gathering dusk toward the other single hut, where the Mothers lived together, apart from the rest of the people. Something inside her felt this was the wrong thing to do, though she could put no words to her feeling.

She turned toward the longhouse, where her own clan lived together. She was of the Bird Clan. That, with the Dog and the Goat Clans, made up the complement of the village, and theirs was the largest of the longhouses.

Inside she found a bedlam of activity, for where so many lived in such close quarters there must be confusion and noise. She moved down the long central corridor to the area allotted to her family. In winter, each family space was screened from the rest with goatskin rugs, which gave privacy to the members and also prevented drafts. But in summer the place was open from front to back, creating a breeze that swept through the doors at either end and carried out the stinks from the tunnel-like building.

With her she brought a handful of green herbs to add to the stewpot her mother tended on the cook fire beyond the farther doorway. Fires burned there in a bare space, their heat and smoke dissipating into the air rather than making the interior of the house uncomfortable.

Her mother was scooping red-hot stones from the edge of her fire with specially shaped sticks and dropping them into her earthenware pots. A great hissing and sizzling greeted each addition to the stew.

Sova looked up as her daughter added the green stuff to her pot. Her smile made a network of wrinkles about her eyes deepen; only those fine brown eyes betrayed the beauty that had been hers, only a few years before.

"You are done with your work?" she asked. "That is good, for I was very tired."

Arma moved the tongs from the pile of stones and said, "You must go and rest now. I will tend the pot, and Father will come soon from the fields with the children. I will see them all fed, and then I shall bring you something to eat."

Sova sighed. "In the old days, I would have been angry to have my daughter cook for me. But now I am relieved. All is not well with me Daughter."

She moved into the house toward her pile of skin-covered straw. Arma looked after her for a moment, knowing, as did Kalva, that her mother would not see another winter. And once Sova was gone, Father would take another woman into the family. At that time Arma would be expected to leave the family's living space.

Already a man from Goat Clan was eyeing her. The Grandmother had passed the word to her parents that she looked favorably upon the match, and once her father took a new wife Arma would be expected to marry, as well.

Already it was late for her to choose a mate, for she was more than twelve summers old. Other girls her age were mothers, already. Yet she did not like to think of taking on the responsibilities of a family. She wanted, instead, to learn what Kalva could teach her and then to minister to her people when the old woman was no longer able to.

She had no desire to tend babies and work hides and weave goat hair into cloth. Any woman could do those things, but Arma felt she had more important tasks ahead of her. She wanted to follow Kalva as herb woman, no matter how much the Grandmother resisted the notion.

Yet she knew her desires were not to be considered in the decisions that would be made for her. On such matters, the Mothers had the final say, and they insisted that all young women must mate and bear children as soon as possible.

Arma sighed, wiping her sweaty forehead on the back of her wrist. If only she were a young man, she thought rebelliously. Even when mated and the fathers of children, the males had a certain amount of free time, once their work in the fields was done.

A woman had no time...hardly was there time to sleep! Every article of clothing everyone wore must be tanned or woven, stitched and shaped. Every bite of food must, in the end, be found, cleaned, and prepared by women.

Arma looked up from the hot stones. In the distance, in the last light of sunset, she could see the dim rank of trees that was the hem of the forest. There had to be more treasures of plants there than numbers of herb women could find and test over many years! Healing and food were there, if they only had the time for finding them. And Kalva was old.

More than anything, Arma realized she would

love to be free to explore those distant reaches of trees and to learn what they held beneath their dark branches. It was, she knew, a traitorous thought, for the tribe was everything. Individual desires counted for nothing, and only the will of the Mother Goddess should be her guide.

Yet deep inside, Arma knew the tribe could survive without her hands or her mind. The Mother Goddess had, indeed, been revealed to her, through the Grandmother, as being more ferocious than loving.

She squashed the thought, but even as she did so she knew she would dearly like to leave the congestion of the village and to move freely through the forest, learning from that vast teacher its lessons of healing and wisdom.

CHAPTER FIVE

SPYING

 BAIN

The boy retreated deep into the forest north of the village, after the girl went away down the path toward her home. A half-day's journey back along his trail he stopped to think about what he had seen.

Before this, the other people had been only tales handed down among hunters and the grandmothers by the cook fires. Now he had seen one of them with his own eyes, as well as an animal that was obviously a friend and a companion of her people.

Though some of the young children among his people kept hares or squirrels, in stick cages, as pets until the family needed them for food, he had never seen any creature that seemed to work with mankind in partnership. This one looked useful, as well as friendly.

Bain climbed into a largish oak tree and sat swinging his legs from one of the thick branches. To have a beast work with you, as that furry one had done with the girl, would be a fine thing, he thought.

Everyone knew animals had sharper senses than the best human hunter could boast of having. That animal had known someone was hiding in a tree above the track; Bain felt that if he had offered any threat to its companion it might well have attacked him.

If his people had such companions guarding their camps, it would be very helpful. No bear or marauding cat or wolf-pack could ever come upon them without warning, given well in advance. It was something to keep in his mind, against a time when he might find a beast suitable for such training.

And the girl—she was different from any he had ever seen. Her dark hair, her rich warm skin, were attractive. She seemed to be more independent than the women to the north, as well, for his mother and sisters and the other women always moved through the forest in large groups, fearful of every animal moving among the trees. This girl seemed to have no fear, as she worked alone.

A bird began its evening song, and he stared up at the sky. The sun was now far down, and he knew he should search for food, for he had not eaten all day. His stomach growled softly, demandingly. He would need energy, if he was to go back tomorrow to watch for the girl or some of her kind once more. He knew he must observe them closely before making any attempt to join them.

He moved through the twilit forest, his eyes searching, his steps silent amid the dead leaves carpeting the ground. Luck was with him, for he clipped a squirrel behind the ear with a stone from his sling. He consumed the raw meat while sitting high in a tree, wondering if he would ever again have the time to make fire and cook a real meal.

His mother did wonderful things with game and roots and leaves from fragrant bushes. Her cakes, which she made with meal she ground from nuts and seeds, made his mouth water, just remembering them. But he seemed doomed, for the time, to raw, wild food, and he knew he was fortunate to have bloody squirrel meat.

At last he curled into a wide space where a branch joined the wide trunk of the tree he had chosen. The sky was now completely dark, and strange sounds wailed and sighed and ratcheted through the wood.

Those had to be the demons the Shaman warned about...lost spirits of hunters who had offended the Horned God, searching for other hunters whose bones had not been put properly to rest.

He shivered. His kilt and cloak were no longer adequate for keeping off the growing chill of early autumn, and he knew he must kill some animal large enough to provide a fur cloak and moccasins. Even though winters were warmer than they had been in his grandfather's childhood, he would need such clothing to keep from freezing, now that he could not depend upon having warm shelter and the comfort of his mother's soft tanned hides.

He woke cramped into a ball, trying to warm his arms between knees and chest. He had trouble straightening himself, and once he slid down from the tree it was difficult to loosen his muscles so they would work properly.

It had been a long while since he had taken the time to bathe in a stream, and he felt dirty. Bark itched in his hair, and his skin was irritated with the bites of insects. He followed the contour of the land to the bottom of a long ridge, and there he found, as he knew he must, a brook purling from a stony hill-side.

He assured himself it was only his desire to be comfortable that made him scrub his hide so hard with a flat stone and comb out his hair so carefully with his fingers. But he kept thinking of the dark-haired girl, who looked very clean and neat in her strange skirt and shawl.

Once he was slicked up, he looked down into a quiet eddy below a boulder and nodded. He looked much better than before, he was certain. She might...but he shook away that thought. He could not decide to try joining her people for a long while yet. If ever.

Birches grew along the stream, and he broke off a twig and chewed the end of it into a brush. With that he scrubbed his teeth vigorously with the sweet, sap-flavored fiber. When he was done he felt more like himself than he had since he ran away from the sacrifice.

Bain moved south again, toward the spot where he had seen the girl. Following a different game trail, he approached from another angle. If there should be any ambush, he would not be caught in it. But no one was in the forest that he could see or hear.

He slipped along the brushy bed of a stream and worked his way, under that cover, more deeply into the flat grasslands. In time, he saw where grass had been torn up into rows of holes, where many odd plants grew. The earth about their roots was dis-turbed, and he could see that weeds and grass had been pulled away to allow the plants to grow unimpeded.

People were working there, gathering into bags green and brown and yellow vegetables from the stalks and bushes and vines. Bain sank into the streambed again to think about what he had seen.

His people gathered wild growing plants, herbs and roots and nuts and fruits, but it had not occurred to them to bring any of those home to plant in a spot that would be both safe and convenient. This was a valuable idea, and he wished he could tell his mother about it. She would find it interesting.

But that made him think of the old Shaman, who would bitterly oppose anyone trying such an unorthodox method. He wanted no change. When Bain's father designed new and better spear points, the Shaman refused to allow them to be used, though all the hunters argued that they would increase their kills.

When the women learned to coat the insides of baskets with mud and bake them over the coals of their fires, upside down, to make leak-proof containers, he threatened and fumed, but the women used them anyway. Women did not fear the Horned God as the hunters must do. They didn't have to go out after game into his dangerous domain.

Bain considered going home to take word of the new and valuable things he had learned, just by watching these strangers. The old man would be furious, he knew, bringing down upon his head not only the wrath of the Horned One but that of the priest's own rage. His defiance had, Bain knew too well, set the ancient afire with fury, as thwarting his will always did.

He sank deeper between the ferny banks of the

stream. He could never go home again. Not to stay...but perhaps he might go near enough to find his sisters gathering nuts in the forest. He could tell them what he had learned, and they could tell their mother.

They would have to pretend to think of these things for themselves. If they mentioned Bain or the girl and her people, even though they were so distant, the Shaman would send hunters again to track him and to kill anyone who was not subject to his wishes and the will of the Horned One.

For a long while Bain lay hidden, watching the people work. Though the men of his tribe would have been embarrassed at working in the forest beside their women, these men showed no shame. All worked together, talking and laughing as if such labor were no burden to them.

Some munched on roots they dug, the bright yellow flesh of which looked good even to Bain. His belly growled, for the squirrel had been used up long ago. When one of the workers turned and approached the stream, however, the boy backed away quietly into the ferns and made his way back into the wood.

He hid in a thicket and almost fell asleep, but he woke to the itch that informs a hunter he is being watched. He opened his eyes and looked about cautiously, moving only his eyes. The girl was sitting on a log beneath a tree, looking interested but not frightened as she stared at him.

She did, however, look wary. He could see she was ready to leap up and run at any sign of a threat, though she was not moving, so far. He relaxed a bit. Moving slowly, he slid out of the thicket to sit on a hummock and stared back at her.

He felt strange. It was something like the feeling he had when he tracked game that could turn dangerous. It was also a bit like the way he felt when he anticipated something good, like a day in the forest with his father.

His stomach was tense, and he was tingling with excitement. He wondered, looking into those wide brown eyes, if she felt the same.

CHAPTER SIX

GOING HOME

Bain sat quite still for a long time, watching the girl, who seemed content to regard him. At last her lips moved, and she smiled. There was no mistaking the expression.

He smiled back, hoping that meant friendship. She reached down to the bag at her feet and took from it one of the yellow roots he had seen the people digging in the field. There were tooth marks at one end, as if she had bitten a chunk out of it. She took another bite, her teeth crunching into the crisp flesh. Then she held out the root to him.

She spoke in an inquiring tone, as he took the root. Bain repeated the sound, staring down at the thing in his hand. "Tur...nip?"

"Good!" The word meant nothing but her tone did. He bit a piece off the root and chewed. It was crisp, fresh-tasting, and tangy. He found he was hungrier than he had thought, and he devoured the entire thing.

The furry animal came out of the bushes and stared at Bain as he ate. The ruff at its neck rose, and it growled much louder than his stomach had been doing, but the girl spoke quietly and put her hand on its back.

She gestured with her other hand toward the creature. "Dog," she said.

That was an easy sound. "Dog," he echoed agreeably.

The dog sat beside the girl, facing the stranger, its tongue lolling from the side of its mouth and drops of saliva drooling down to drip on the dusty grass at its feet. Its gaze never left him, and Bain thought if he offered a threat to the girl the creature would certainly be at his throat with all the ferocity of a wolf.

Bain felt a shiver run down his back. Those teeth were not nearly as long or as sharp as those of a wolf, but they looked capable of tearing out his throat without any trouble at all.

He rose, careful not to move so quickly that he might alarm the animal. He felt about in his pouch, which he wore tied about his waist beneath his kilt. His few treasures were there, and a gift demanded a gift in return.

The rule was inflexible among his people, and it never occurred to him that he might take something from her without giving in return.

He searched through the contents of the pouch to find the bright pebble he had found in a stream far in the north. It sparkled and shone in the light, its cream and pink colors glowing in the sunlight. He had always thought it very beautiful.

His fingers curled about its rounded shape,

which was warm from the heat of his skin. It had comforted him in darkness. Perhaps this alien woman might also find comfort in it. The Shaman— he almost smiled at the thought—would be furious if he knew Bain had offered a gift to a stranger, no matter what the reason might be.

He shrugged. The old man would never know, for he hoped never to see his withered face again, even if it meant a lonely death in the forest. He held out the stone.

The sun struck it, bringing to light all its glimmers. She stared at it, her face brightening. Then, rising, she reached for the pebble.

"A gift for a gift," said Bain, and she seemed to understand his meaning, if not his words.

Cupping it in her hands, she lifted it to the light. She laughed aloud and lifted her own pouch, which swung from a cord to the string holding her skirt, and placed the pebble inside it.

The dog rose and stared toward the field beyond the arm of trees. He growled softly. It was not a threat but a communication to the girl.

"I must go," she said, gesturing toward the village. "This is a wonderful gift. Thank you."

Bain had no trouble understanding her meaning, although the words were alien to him. As she moved away, he wondered if he would ever see her again. Once she was out of sight, he climbed into a tree again and thought even harder than before.

This spot was so different from his own country it was hard to believe it was only a double handful of days journey from his old home. Already he had learned things that would be valuable to his kin, if they could know of them and if the Shaman would allow them to use them.

As long as the old man lived, that might be impossible, but he was ancient. He would not live forever, and Andia, his apprentice, was a man of broader mind than his mentor. He might well, in years to come, open the ways of the People to new and better things.

If he could only tell his sisters or his mother of these new ways, they could, if nothing else, keep them secretly in their minds until it was safe to mention them. Bain ached to take the trail northward and carry these valuable secrets to his people.

He glanced toward the village, which showed only as a column of smoke beyond the trees. The Horned One had sent him here, he felt certain, to learn of these new methods of living. Now he must go very quietly, very secretly, back to his own village and find someone to tell them to.

He knew he would not mention these people in the south, though his kin would know he must have met some of the other kinds in his travels. No hint must reach the Shaman of these strangers less than a moon's journey from his own place.

Bain would remain only long enough to pass on the information he had been sent to gather, and then he would flee into the forest. Perhaps he might go eastward, toward those mountains that loomed on the horizon. He would survive as long as possible. It was unlikely he would ever come this way again, for nothing must exist to lead the Shaman's hunters into these lands.

Yet he felt some bit of him would remain here with that dark-haired girl, somehow caught and preserved in the stone in her pouch.

Bain set out toward the north, hoping the Horned One would not lead anyone else here, for he felt the hunters and the farmers would not greet each other with kindness. Clashes with other hunting clans, met only at great intervals when game grew scarce and desperation sent hunters out of their own territories, had given him a distaste for blood. He wanted no such battles between his own people and those belonging to his new friend.

Moving through the forest again, as the trees grew larger, their thickness greater, he found himself wondering if anyone still searched the wood for him. Had the Shaman actually sent searchers after him, as he had done in the past when dealing with those who flouted the god, with orders to return with his body or not at all?

His father had told him of such hunts and the men who had been brought back dead after terrible fighting. If such a group ranged the forest, searching for him under such orders, he had best go even more cautiously.

Bain felt he could find his mother or sisters as they ranged the fall forest near the village, seeking fallen nuts and medicinal roots. Their habits were regular, and he knew their herb patches and favorite nut-trees as well as they.

He felt his belly shrink at the thought of being captured, but he knew the Horned One had meant for him to go and to come again. He did not flinch from his task by day, but at night, as he slept high in the tops of trees, he dreamed ill dreams.

CHAPTER SEVEN

THE GRANDMOTHER

☼ARMA☼

Arma was gathering water-growing plants along the stream when Roff cocked his ears and stared off toward the trees. The girl took her bundle of dripping roots and leaves to the drying shed before heading for the wood herself to look for the boy, who must, she thought, be hiding there, watching her people work. She took the turnip from a pile, as a gift for him, as she finished her task at the healer's hut.

No one thought anything of her going, for she worked in the forest much of the time, finding and gathering both old and new herbs. She had said nothing of her encounter to anyone but Kalva, and as nothing had been done about it she hoped everything was secure.

Her second glimpse of him she mentioned to no one, feeling her duty had been done with that first report. What happened now was her own business. And there was something about the half-starved lad that roused her interest.

Kalva, however, was an old woman who was wise in the nature of her people. As soon as Arma dropped the armload of wood she brought back from her trek to the forest, the healer murmured, "So, the boy is back."

Arma was stunned. The pebble was hidden in her pouch, she knew, invisible to anyone except the intuition of her mentor. She sighed.

"I sometimes think you have more power than the Mothers, Kalva. How did you know I saw the boy in the wood?" she asked.

Kalva cackled. "You come back from gathering wood with your eyes sparkling and your cheeks pink and expect me to believe the trees excited you so? Take care, young one. Strangers can be dangerous, even when they seem harmless.

"Even those who mean no harm go away, at last, or they remain to make trouble. Stick to your own kind, I advise you, and let strangers go back to theirs."

Arma felt herself blushing. Why did that pale-haired boy with eyes like patches of blue sky interest her, while the man from Goat Clan had never roused in her anything but amused distaste?

She felt suddenly protective, though she knew he had to be strong and clever to survive alone in the forest. It was not merely the fact that he looked different, she thought. There was something inside the boy that echoed her own spirit. From the look in his eyes when he gave her the pebble, she felt this to be true.

She said no more, but on the next day she went among the trees, digging stick in hand. She looked for him, but there was no trace or whisper of his presence, and Roff gave no sign that anyone might be hiding in a treetop.

Arma felt rather ruffled. Kalva was right; strangers let you become fond of them and then disappeared like a dream.

Or was he one of the forest demons in the tales her people told about the fires at night? The deep forests of the north, said the old ones, were filled with evil spirits whose shrill voices echoed through the night. Even the animals living in those lands were terrifying, and more than one who had been sent to explore the north had never returned to the village.

A few had come back in a handful of days, claiming that if they had pursued their quest they never would have found their way home at all. They told of weird sounds in the night, the wailings of monsters even more fearful than those they saw by day.

Arma wondered how the boy, all alone, traveled where armed men either died or retreated to safety. Where were his people—or what were his people? Or was he a demon disguised as a human person?

Arma shook herself and pushed such nonsensical ideas away. She put her hand into her pouch and felt the pink pebble. He was kind, and he had given her the finest thing he had, she was certain. Good manners showed he had been reared well, whoever his people might be.

She put him out of her mind as she worked. Three young children were ill of a fever. Kalva needed the bark of certain trees growing along the streams in the forest and certain roots the girl knew to exist deeper among the trees. When Arma had collected the necessary ingredients, she hurried back to help Kalva prepare the thick and bitter teas with which she dosed this particular illness.

Arma took turns all the night, sitting up with Kalva and the children's mother to tend them and to administer the doses of the medicine. Though the small patients protested, morning found their fever broken, and the girl returned, heavy-eyed, toward Kalva's hut.

As she went, she was summoned to the Grandmother. No matter how weary she might be, she could not ignore such a message, for the Grandmother was the eldest, the wisest, and the nearest to the Mother Goddess of all the Mothers of the tribe.

Yawning and shivering together, Arma went to the large hut where the Mothers lived and tapped on the stone doorstep.

"Come, child," wheezed an ancient voice from within. "Tell me your story. Kalva has told me once, but now I want to hear all you know about this intruder into our country."

The girl shivered again, harder. Would the Grandmother know if she were told only a part of the truth? Would it be possible to conceal her most recent meeting with the boy in the wood? All her life she had been taught that the Mothers detected any lie instantly, but could they distinguish a partial truth from a complete one?

If nothing else, Arma was determined to conceal the gift of her pebble. The Grandmother would take it away and use it to draw the giver into her clutches, the girl knew. That would be a sorry return for such a beautiful gift.

She stooped to enter the dark room and sank to her knees beside the bench on which the old woman sat. Bending her head reverently, she said, "I serve you, Grandmother."

"Eh! Eh! So you do, but enough of that. Tell me of the creature you saw in the trees."

The ancient face gleamed like oiled leather in the dim light from the doorway. In that network of wrinkles, her black eyes shone, though one of them was partially glazed with a milky film. A skinny hand shot out and caught Arma's wrist.

"Now tell me everything!"

The grip on her wrist was painful, the stick-like fingers cutting into her flesh. Something inside Arma flared into rebellion. What right had this old woman to treat her so, as if she had done something wrong?

She was no part of Arma's secret or her life. She had no right to anything, the girl felt suddenly, except the reverence owed to the old. Yet she knew better than to show her reaction. She sank onto her heels on the chill dirt of the floor and began to speak. The old woman's grasp did not slacken on her wrist, and sometimes she squeezed painfully.

Arma wanted to protest, but she didn't dare. Somehow, selecting her words with great care, she told her tale to the end.

The bony face bent close to her own. "The dog, now, he didn't bark? He would bark at an animal, I should think."

Arma looked up in astonishment. Surely she had made it clear that this was a human boy she was describing. Was the old woman mad, now, in her dotage?

"It was no animal but a human person, not much older than I, I should think. He was like the traders I have been told of who used to come to our village back in the old days on the coast."

"Tell me again how he looked." A gust of foul breath washed over her face, and Arma felt her stomach quease. And that almost betrayed her into too great a familiarity with the look of the stranger, for only in her lengthy visit with him had she been able to observe him closely. When first she saw him he was half concealed among the leaves of the high branches.

She caught herself in time. "He seemed rather tall and thin, what I could see of him. I would say that he was young, a boy not a man. His skin looked very pale, and his hair was the first thing that caught my eye. It shone golden in the sunlight."

"Our people have dark hair," said the Grandmother.

"But my grandmother told me of the northern traders who came by sea. She said they were tall and fair, and their hair was like sunlight. No one denied that they were men."

"I do," said the old woman. "They were covered with fur. I remember them, for I saw them as a small child. Like bears, they were, more than like men. Ridiculous creatures!" Her mouth closed like a trap, making her nose almost touch her chin. Her black eyes observed Arma closely.

The girl took a deep breath, calming herself. "Roff didn't bark once. He saw him and warned me, but he didn't give a single indication that this person might be dangerous."

"And all alone, because of a dog, you decided

this was no enemy! Foolishness! You should have called at once for the men to come and catch him. A creature of that sort would make a fine sacrifice to the Mother Goddess at full moon."

Something inside Arma congealed into a cold lump. She hated the spring and fall sacrifices, even though she only heard of them from her married peers. She dreaded the time when she must take a mate and go to perform part of those bloody rituals with the other women of the village.

The idea frightened her. The thudding of the drums, which could be heard even inside the long-house, safe with her family, gave her gooseflesh, and the shrill voices chanting made her shiver.

But she kept her wits about her. "He is gone now, I am sure. Probably back into the forest where he came from. Now it is too late." Despite her efforts, Arma found her voice a bit unsteady.

Desperately, she pushed back her thoughts about the sacrifices, for the Grandmother seemed, at times, almost to read the minds of her people. Blasphemy of the sort she had just felt had been known to bring people to grief as sacrifices.

The Grandmother's grip was entirely too strong for such a skinny hand. She seemed to be thinking deeply. "I will send the men," she said at last. "They will find him, if he is still nearby, and if not they will track him and catch him. There will be time before full moon to secure such a suitable sacrifice. Go and show them where you saw this person."

The hand relaxed, and Arma rubbed her bruised wrist.

"Go now and Chass will go with you, taking enough men for the task. Then return to Kalva once you have showed them the spot. And think, young Arma, about taking a mate. I have approved the one, and now you must accept him, or you will be punished."

Arma backed out of the hut and stood, shaking, her teeth clenched to keep them from chattering. She had, in those few moments in the forest, accepted that boy as a friend. And now, in this short time with the Grandmother, she knew the old woman was her bitter enemy, who ordered her to betray him.

Chass returned from conferring with the Grandmother and said, "Come with us, now."

Weary and angry, the girl turned to follow him. She could only obey, no matter how she hated the thought of what must follow.

CHAPTER EIGHT

LOSING MOTHER

☼SOVA☼

Three more men fell in behind her as Arma moved up the path behind Chass. As they went into the trees, Arma felt a strange sickness at being forced to lead them to the spot where she had first seen the stranger, and she was glad that Roff had remained behind in Kalva's hut.

It was odd—the little dog refused to go near the hut belonging to the Mothers, even when Kalva visited it. When she had turned in that direction, after her long night of nursing, the dog growled and retreated behind Kalva. That was good, for if he had been with those now hunting the boy he might well give better guidance than Arma intended to do.

She found herself hoping that the stranger had gone very far, very fast. No one, whoever he might be, deserved to die at the hands of the Grandmother.

Once they were well into the wood, she paused to look about. "It was here where I first caught a glimpse of his hair shining—up in that tree over there." She pointed not to the tree in which he had hidden, but one near it.

The men of her tribe were neither hunters nor trackers, and she felt that Chass would never find any traces clear enough to prove her a liar. He grunted and sent the men to examine the tree she indicated. One even climbed up it and scurried around in the branches like some oversized squirrel. The remaining pair dropped to hands and knees and examined the ground for tracks.

Of course there was nothing. Even if it had been the correct tree, Arma knew that the weather would have destroyed any traces, and besides that young man knew enough about the wild to live there alone. He would probably never leave a track that the inexpert eyes of her own kind could detect.

Chass mused for a moment. "We will cast back and forth through the wood and we may find some trace of him. You can go now, Arma."

She backed away and then turned to run toward the village. Tears were spilling over her cheeks, and she wiped them on the back of her wrist as she ran.

She managed to gain control before she reached Kalva's hut, where she entered quietly and took up her task of keeping hot stones in the pot to simmer the medicinal herbs. Once that was done, she slept for a time, before a shout waked her. Someone called her name from the direction of the longhouse, and she went, yawning, to see what was needed.

Kiri, her youngest sister, was running toward her. Something in the way the child moved filled Arma's heart with dread.

"Mother," Kiri shouted, her small legs pumping as hard as she could send them. "Oh come, Arma,

Mother wants you. She's sick!"

The girl's body went still with pain. Kalva came from the hut and nodded for her to run, and she set off as fast as she could, knowing the old woman would come after her. She scooped Kiri up in her arms as she reached her and carried her quickly on to the longhouse.

Down its length she ran and out the other end into the arc of fires kept burning for cooking. Sova lay beside her fire, the bone ladle clutched tightly in her hand, her knuckles pale with the pressure. Her face was even more pale, its wrinkles dark, as if traced with ashes.

Arma knelt and lifted her mother into her arms. "We will take you to the sleeping mat," she said. "Kalva will make you a tea that will help you to get well." But she knew even as she spoke that she was lying.

Sova let the ladle drop and Kiri caught it. "Stir the food," she gasped. "Your father and the others... will be hungry!"

Kiri nodded gravely and began to stir the pot, though the stones had cooled and it was no longer bubbling. Arma turned away, her mother's slight weight caught closely in her arms. Without feeling the burden, she took Sova into the longhouse to the family space.

When she eased the woman onto her own sleeping mat, the girl knelt beside her, holding her thin, calloused hand. Kalva came quickly to kneel opposite her, touching Sova's forehead for a long moment. Then she took both her hands and leaned to sniff at her skin. She looked very grave.

Arma stared across her mother's shrunken

shape. Kalva's dark eyes were sad as she stroked Sova's face with a gentle hand. "Goodbye, old friend," she said.

Sova managed a tiny smile. "Service with the Mother Goddess will not, I think, be any harder than that I have done here all my life," she whispered. "I am so weary, Kalva."

She turned her gaze to her daughter. "Arma, you must not feel responsible for the children, for your father will choose Roma to mother them, I am sure. And"—she glanced once questioningly at Kalva before continuing—"do not feel that because a man looks longingly at you, you must look back at him. The Grandmother told us to make you marry into Goat Clan.

"That is sad. Willing service to a family is hard enough, but when one's heart is not in it, surely it would break the strongest spirit. Search your heart, my daughter. I have always thought you must have some special fate other than the one I found."

The dying woman's eyes widened as she stared into the dimness of the longhouse. "I see...there are other answers than those we know. Ours are not the only ways, and perhaps you will find...a new one." But now her breath was gone, and no more came. The blankness of death glazed her eyes.

Arma laid her hand over her mother's heart, finding no throb there. "She can rest now," she said. "She was so very tired. But what did she mean, there at the last?"

Kalva was staring as if into the depths of her own mind and spirit. She came back slowly to answer her apprentice. "It is not for me to say. Yet I, too, have seen glimpses of other answers than those the Mothers teach.

"I have heard strange words carried on the breeze at midnight. I have...."—she caught her breath—"No. What she meant is that you must listen to your own mind and learn for yourself what you must do. One who cannot do that does best to remain within the security of the Goddess and the Clan."

Arma sighed and helped the healer clean her mother's body and wrap her in the skins she most valued. Tomorrow there would be a ritual, and she would be put into a long barrow, along with her pots and ladles, her bone needles and other implements. She would need them all, in the land beyond death.

When all was done, Arma sat waiting for her father and the other children to come from the fields. Her life was about to change, completely and permanently, and this would be her last time in this space where she had been born.

The girl felt frightened. Even Kalva could not help her now, for her life was in the hands of the Grandmother. And Arma knew better than ever before that the old woman did not mean her well.

CHAPTER NINE

BEING HUNTED

 BAIN

Although he was traveling briskly through the forest, Bain was thinking all the while of those people behind him at the village amid fields of food plants. This would be valuable information; he knew that his mother and sisters could bring rootstocks of useful plants from the forest and set them into the space behind their hut. That would mean that no one would have to risk her life hunting for them in the wood.

But all the while he saw, behind his eyes, the picture of the girl and her animal. Her bright black eyes and the flipping tail of hair that swung behind her were unusual and he thought that no girl of his own tribe had ever caught his eye so.

Then he realized that he was not watching carefully as he moved through the trees. To travel in the forest he needed to be fully alert, and he forced himself to concentrate upon the path, the depths of the wood, the sounds and the scents that would warn him of danger.

He thought about seeing his mother again without distraction. She would be happy, if fearful, to find him nearby, and she would listen to him, he knew. Though she feared the Shaman, she did not revere him, and he knew she would find a way to spread this new way of making food to the other families.

She would not hand her son to the Shaman, he was certain. The old man would not forget his blasphemy, and he still probably had men searching the forest to find him and drag him back to punishment. His rages were such that even the bravest of the hunters dared not face them.

No, if he still had searchers out after him, they would not return without him, if catching him seemed possible at all. If it took them all winter, they would continue their hunt. If he hoped to survive this visit to his home, he knew he must go with great skill and greater caution.

He shivered, trotting along a game track between lines of bushes. He knew he should not risk this journey, and yet he felt in his heart that it had been for this purpose the great stag had sent him southward. He could not waste that. But what he would do, once the information passed into his mother's keeping, he did not know.

A single man in the forest was terribly vulnerable, for he could not keep watch while he slept, and no one could remain awake forever. There were no eyes and ears to keep focused both before and behind. In the world of the forest, that could mean the difference between life and death.

A sound caught his ear, and he stopped in his

tracks, silent, listening hard. Something moved in the undergrowth, somewhat to his right and behind him.

He knew with sudden certainty that a large animal was tracking him. He could go up a tree at once and be safe for the time being, but at last he would have to come down again. He could not remain there forever, and many predators could wait out even the most determined prey that took cover in a treetop.

Bain remained still, his mind racing as he reviewed his choices. He was weary of running and hiding and climbing to escape danger. If he could not kill the animal that stalked him, then he would submit to being killed by it. All his problems would end with that, and he would be content.

He held his short spear tightly in his right hand, fumbling in the sling beneath his kilt after the flint knife that he carried at his waist. Once it was solidly in his fist, he moved forward, still listening.

He heard padding paws on the mulchy trail behind him, and he slowed deliberately, balanced against any sudden attack. He was tense, ready to move in any direction at an instant's notice.

The big gray wolf launched himself from the cover of a clump of berry bushes. Bain whirled, his spear held ready, going down onto one knee. The wide mouth, fanged with dagger-like teeth, was aimed at his throat, but instead it was pierced by a sharp spear-point of flint.

The weight of the animal, as it slid down the shaft onto him, pushed Bain backward onto the path. The boy clung to the staff, pushing himself back, out from beneath the flailing wolf, still keeping the spear-shaft wedged against the ground, though blood made the wood slick and hard to hold.

The beast gave a howl that was half a gurgle, and its paws scrabbled at the dirt, still trying to move the dying body toward its victim. Even in the midst of its pain it held to its purpose, and such was its weight and strength that it knocked the spear sideways, sending Bain down with the wolf on top of him.

But his other hand was busy with the knife, stabbing frantically at the side and the neck of the beast, whose hot breath was now in his face, making him feel faint and sick. The stench of the animal was terrible, made worse by the scent of its blood, whose hot flood covered his arm and shoulder. Then the beast shuddered and sank, its full weight on top of the boy.

Bain lay beneath that terrible weight, panting, trying to catch his breath. Then he squirmed, digging in his heels, worming his way out from under the body, all coated with dust and blood. He stared down; the body twitched, as if still hungering after his flesh.

The gray pelt was already thickening for winter, and he knew he would need a warm fur if he intended to survive the cold months without a roof over his head. He had earned this hide, his first solitary big kill. He determined at that moment to skin out the wolf and scrape the pelt, here and now, though he had no time to cure the skin properly.

Dragging the carcass, he hunted downhill until he found a brook. There he washed himself clean and rinsed out his kilt and his cloak. Then he got to work in earnest.

Before nightfall he had skinned the animal, with much difficulty, for his knife was not keen. He scraped the flesh and the fat away from the leather before cracking the skull to extract the brain, with which he scrubbed the inside of the pelt thoroughly. He pegged the hide out high in a tree so that scavengers could not reach it to spoil it.

The flesh of the animal was rank and tasted terrible, but he chewed it anyway, swallowing the bloody juices. He needed the strength it would give him, and perhaps some of the ferocity of the wolf would not come amiss, now that he was on his own.

He spent the night on a branch above the wide span of trunk to which he had fastened his trophy. The dark hours were noisy with the shrieks and growls of the scavengers finishing the wolf's carcass, but he slept well, waking only when the worst of the howls rose to his treetop. Even the stink of the pelt could not keep him awake.

When light touched the sky, he climbed down and unfastened the skin. Taking it to the side of the stream, he washed out the brains, though he knew it was too soon, and scrubbed the inner layer with damp sand. By the time he pounded dry sand into the damp hide, shook it out, pounded it in again, he knew that his work was passable, though not good.

He scraped it out once more with his flint knife. By now it was late afternoon, and he was sick of the stink of the thing, but he persevered until he knew that the skin was as well cleaned as he could make it, without taking more time than he had to do it.

He tied the pelt to the tree and washed himself again. Then he went to hunt grubs and berries for his growling belly. The next morning he began shaping the wolf skin into a cloak, making a hood of the head of the animal, carefully skinned away from the skull that he had removed. Below the head skin, the huge hide hung in loose folds, and he trimmed it so that it would not drag awkwardly on the ground.

His treatment had cleaned it enough so that he could try it on, and it covered him almost like a tent. Two like him could have shared its shelter on a cold night, and he was pleased to know that he had such a useful garment with which to go into the winter.

He moved well away from the scene of all his work, taking the skin with him. There was still some of the beast left, farther up the bank of the stream, and small fierce cats came to quarrel over it as soon as he was out of sight, though he could hear their snarls and growls for a long distance as he went.

This time he tied the wolf skin high in his sleeping tree, once he found one to suit him, and downwind, to keep the smell from bothering him. In time, it would dry. If he could find a place and the leisure to work it, he could scuff out any stiffness with scraping stones, ashes, and effort.

"Bain," he said to himself softly. "Wolf-Killer." He settled into his sleeping tree, thinking how fine it would feel if ever again he had the chance to sleep on a pile of dried grasses, safe inside a shelter, covered with warm furs. Sleeping high in a tree was the safe thing to do, but no one could call it comfortable.

He woke just before dawn. Some sound, some scent, something had pulled him out of his dream, and he lay still, listening hard. Then he knew. Voices sounded, quiet but distinct, off to the east of his perch.

He strained his ears, trying to identify those voices. They could not belong to any of his own people, for they knew better than to talk aloud in the forest. They signaled with their hands, or they whistled like any of the many birds that thronged there, using codes that all understood. These were not, he knew, any searchers sent out by the Shaman.

Sliding down silently to the ground beneath his tree, he crept eastward through the forest. At last he lay flat, hidden in a thicket, watching the trail running north and south. That was the one along which he had traveled.

In a bit three men came walking along it, their steps thudding on the ground, their bodies crackling the bushes that leaned out over the track. They were short men, dark like those he had watched in the fields beside that village in the south.

Why were they here, approaching the territory of his own people? He had seen no one except the girl, and he did not believe she would set such men on his track.

What did these strangers intend to do in this world that belonged to the hunters of the north?

CHAPTER TEN

BETWEEN TWO ENEMIES

☼BAIN☼

Listening to their trampling, Bain realized that these people knew little about woodcraft. If they were after game, they would never find it, whatever it might be. And if they were after him...he found it impossible to take them seriously as enemies.

Yet they were moving north, as he had come, and if they went on as they were, in a few days they would come into the tribal hunting grounds. Knowing the Shaman as he did, Bain shuddered. He would make war on these clumsy southerners, that was a certainty.

Worse yet, some of his own people might die. His younger brother, Dar, was now old enough to hunt, and the thought that he might be one who fell made the boy feel an empty sickness inside himself.

Whatever the danger, Bain knew he must warn his clan that strangers walked the forest. He could not let them risk surprise at the hands of these newcomers. Rising silently, he slid away through the trees, moving so quickly that their voices soon faded into the distance.

He climbed high and hid his precious wolf skin, marking the spot in his memory so that he could return, if he had the chance, to find his trophy. Then he ran, avoiding the game trails, which those awkward men behind him would be sure to use because they were plainly marked by the prints of deer and wild pigs and other animals.

The trees of the forest had become huge again as he came north, and their spreading branches shaded the forest floor beneath them, leaving little undergrowth. He sped through, risking coming upon a belated bear or cat, until he could run no more.

For two days he went like the wind, stopping for nothing except a few hours of exhausted sleep. When he drew near his old home again, however, he slowed his pace. That was as well, for in the late morning he crept through a tangle and saw, among the trees forming a small spinney in the distance, a glint of pale hair caught in a sunbeam.

Lying still in a tangle of bushes and vines, he watched as a group of his own people came closer, their route angling south and east. They were obviously searching for sign, for Kawn, the best tracker of all, bent almost double, keeping his gaze busy sweeping the ground. His first impulse was to run to them, to warn them that danger might come through the forest. But he held himself in check, knowing that those were dedicated servants of the Horned God, directed by the Shaman. They would not believe the word of one who had committed sacrilege.

They came on, safely to one side of his position, and they halted at last within earshot of the boy. Lying in his covert, he heard a familiar voice say, "How is it that Bain came so far, if indeed he did? At first the Shaman was sure that he hid near the village, but we have searched every hand span of forest for a day's march about it.

"We are farther from our homeplace than anyone has gone from our tribe, and still there is neither track nor sign. The Horned One has taken him." Kesh, who had been his father's friend, was the speaker.

"If the Horned One has not punished him as yet, he will certainly do that, once the Shaman takes the young man into his hands," said another, his voice carefully neutral. That one had been his own friend, Eshwa, Bain realized.

Kawn laughed. "He will be lucky if he is already with the god. The Shaman had his heart set upon making him the Hunter for this next seven years, for there is no other suitable young hunter. He has declared old Clar's son Dep the Hunter, now, but the child is only ten winters old."

Bain felt a chill at his heart. He knew Dep, a jolly little fellow, already showing great promise. To force a child to become Hunter for the tribe was terrible and foolish, he felt. And to kill him when he had fewer than two double handfuls of summers to his count was cruel.

The old man must be losing his wits. In seven years, just as he was caring for a young family of his own, the boy would be strangled, as Bain's father had been, bound to the ancient oak in the glade. He would be sent to the Horned One—and that thought brought another.

Bain had seen the Horned One, and he had not

been angry. Instead, he had sent his rebellious subject on a journey that ended in important discover-
ies. No, he had other uses for his servants, and the
old Shaman, it was now clear, served no purpose but
his own. He certainly did not speak for the god!

Bain buried himself carefully in his tangle and
lay still and silent as the men rested and rose to continue their search. Only when they had passed him
did he remember that they would, if they continued
southward, probably meet those dark southerners.

He shivered, remembering how the Shaman had
taught the clans to hate and fear strange people,
whatever their intentions might be. He knew now
that strangers were not devils and demons, as the
Shaman had described them, but, despite their different looks and ways, not unlike anyone else.
These men, most older than he, would be frightened
when they met the dark ones.

Kesh would look at the black hair and the brown
skins and say, "But the Shaman is right. This is not
the look of Man. Kill them!"

What then? Bain felt a guess burning inside him,
for the Shaman hated even his own kind. How much
more he would hate those who were unlike the
hunter clans!

There would be killing, when his people's hunters met the strangers, and he could not warn either
group. His own would capture him, without listening to his warnings. The others would not understand his words, and they would likely kill him at
once.

However, he found that he must know what was
happening, and he crept stealthily after the hunters,
following them south and east to parallel his track.

He blessed the instinct that had told him to avoid the trails, for they would have found his spoor, no matter how faint it might be.

They would have sensed his presence with that strange instinct that hunters develop, unless they die too quickly. He thought gratefully of his wolf skin, which had changed his own smell so that even one of Kesh's men might not recognize his scent if he caught a whiff of it in the wood. He would know Man. He might not recognize Bain.

He found that he had, in his haste, come farther than he thought. For two days he kept the searchers within earshot, and he hid and rested high in the trees when they camped for the night. As they went, they cast about for some sign of him, sometimes dispersing through the trees to widen their search.

It made him sick to think of those keen eyes, those sensitive ears hunting for him. Why should men hunt their own kind? Why should the Shaman feel so much threat at the thought of other human beings sharing his world?

There came a sharp cry in the distance, a signal. Not from his own, for they communicated in whistles and chirps, but from that other group, he was sure. The two parties had sighted each other!

He sped through the wood until he could hear confused sounds ahead. Then he climbed the tallest tree he could find and looked down over the forest below its crown.

Two of the hunters ran as fast as they could, heading toward the south. The third went into the trees, angling toward the track the strangers followed. Beyond, he could make out the bobbing specks that were three black-haired heads as they moved away quickly.

He had not thought that men who dug in the ground might run so very fast, but they were leaving his own people behind them. Even as he stared, the last went out of sight into the thickness of the wood. If they held that pace and did not tire too quickly they might reach their own village in far less time than it had taken him, walking and pausing to rest, to go there.

He caught his breath. Kesh was turning back, still running, as the other two pursued the strangers. There could be only one reason—the others would mark the trail and keep the prey in sight. Kesh would go back and tell the Shaman of their discovery.

Then, Bain was certain, he would send many hunters to destroy these strangers who could not be servants of the Horned God. He felt cold and frightened, for he knew the Shaman too well, and he had watched these people as they worked peacefully in their fields.

Men killed men, he had known all his life, over game that both claimed for their kills or over a woman or when drinking the brew of berries and wild seeds. Did groups of men also kill each other, simply because they were different?

He felt cold and sick at the thought.

CHAPTER ELEVEN

OUT OF THE TREES

☼ARMA☼

It had been days since Chass and his men had left the village, and Arma was disturbed. Each time she went into the wood to gather herbs and roots she watched and listened, thinking she might hear some sound that might tell her they were returning.

They might have come to grief in the forest, she knew, and that would be a sad loss to her people. But she also hated to think they might return with a bright-haired captive for the Grandmother's sacrifice.

When they came at last she was not in the forest but busy tending the fire for Kalva. For now she slept sheltered in a tiny lean-to against the side of the herb woman's hut. Roma had come into her family's part of the house to share her father's sleeping place, and that left no room for a grown daughter.

Twice the Mother had called Arma into the hut she shared with the Grandmother and the Daughter, and twice the stern trio had talked to her of her duty. She must accept a mate and bring new babies into the clan, they told her, but something inside the girl had rebelled and continued to rebel.

When she pleaded that she was not yet a woman, they ignored the argument. "Very soon you will become one," the Grandmother told her, those bright dark eyes sparkling in the dim light of the hut. "You must accept your life, as we decide it. You have lived for thirteen summers, and very soon you will begin your life as a woman. Another can become apprentice to the herb woman in your place."

That thought hurt worse than anything else. Arma loved her work, and she loved Kalva. Leaving either would be painful, but the thought of leaving both made her hot with fury. However, she kept that in her heart, as she also did those other words she must not reveal.

"I hate the man from Goat Clan," she would have loved to say. "I shudder when he looks at me, and I never go near him when I can avoid it." She knew, all too well, that none of the Mothers would listen, even if she spoke, or would care, even if they understood her feelings.

The only reason she had been allowed to take more time was because Kalva had spoken for her before the Mothers. The tribe, everyone knew, must have a healer, and the old woman had stood firmly before those powerful women and insisted upon a delay.

"No woman who is busy with her own family can find the time to learn what must be taught to her," Kalva said to the sour old woman. "I will not live for many years, for I am growing old. There has been no woman with the ability I need for my apprentice, except for this one.

"When I am gone, you will need someone to find medicinal plants and to test them. You will need one who knows how to concoct the potions and brews that cure fevers and infections that trouble our people. When sick children cry at your door, you will think of this, if you force this child into marriage now."

Grudgingly the Mothers had granted a delay until such time as another child showed a gift for healing. As there was no room in Kalva's hut for anyone except her, Arma had tied brush into a slanting roof and rolled herself beneath it in a skin blanket, grateful even for such slight shelter.

The fire before the door was kept burning all night, since she took up residence, and often she rose in the night to add a chunk of wood to the glowing coals. Even so, she missed the warmth and closeness of her family's place in the great house of her clan.

She was putting fresh stones in the pot one morning when she looked up to see Chass and his group burst from the line of trees and head for the hut of the Mothers. They ran, she knew with sudden certainty, as if they were frightened, pursued from the forest by some dangerous foe. She had never before known Chass to fear anything at all.

"Kalva!" she called into the dark hut behind her, "the searchers are back, and they seem afraid. Come and see!"

The old woman stooped beneath the low doorway and stared toward the other hut. Chass had just reached it and was dropping to his knees in order to crawl into that cramped space. Behind him, his companions sank onto the ground, their chests heaving with effort. They looked often toward the wood from which they had come, as if fearing pursuit.

Kalva nodded. "They have found more than they looked for," she said, her tone wry. "They followed that boy you saw, and I suspect they stirred up his folk, wherever they live up there in the great forest.

"We have lived here in safety for too many generations, now. The Mothers have forgotten what it was like when we were attacked by other tribes, there in the south. My grandmother told me tales of such battles, and they made ill hearing."

She laid aside the herbs she had brought to add to the pot to steep for a cough remedy. Returning to her hut, she brought out a great deal of bark and roots and leaves, which she proceeded to drop into the pot in their place, measuring the amounts she added very carefully.

Turning to Arma, the herb woman said, "Go to the swampy spot in the stream and find those soft mosses that grow there. They are good for stopping the bleeding of wounds. Unless I am badly mistaken, we shall need such matters before this is settled."

The girl took a woven grass bag and moved quickly to do as she was told, though that was a hard thing. She wanted to run to Urlo and ask if he had seen the boy, but she knew that there would be no reply until the Mothers gave permission.

The walk was short, and she found a large patch of the moss and filled her bag quickly. Kalva was still tending the pot of medicine when she returned.

The old woman was glancing, Arma saw as she approached, toward the Mothers' house frequently.

Urlo and Grep lounged on the grass, so Chass had not yet come out. It looked as if the pair had dropped off to sleep, exhausted with their running.

"He has brought very bad news," the old woman said, as Arma set the bag of moss in the shade of the hut and dampened it from a pot of water to keep it fresh. "I believe that the Grandmother made a terribly bad decision when she sent them after that boy." She gave the pot an angry stir.

"We will all suffer for that, I think. But you may want to speak to your father and the children. Things can change, my child, very quickly and...." —she sighed, as if remembering something very sad—"and permanently. Run, now, and speak to your family."

Arma felt stunned with surprise. She had known a feeling of unease since the searchers left, but it had not occurred to her that the party might bring so much danger in their wake. What sort of people might be on their way, even now, toward her village?

She turned and ran to the field where her father and Roma and the young ones worked with their digging sticks. She stumbled past piles of turnips and other root-crops as she headed for the family's plot.

Her father looked up as she approached, straightening to wait for her to draw near. From his stance she knew that he felt something was wrong.

"Kalva has sent me to speak to you," she panted. "She says...that Chass and his men...have brought danger with them...from the north!"

With one motion, her father signaled for his brood to cluster near him, as she went on, "Go back to the village, Father, and...call to the others in the fields. They may not listen...to me. Tell them to go home quickly.

"Something...is about to happen!"

CHAPTER TWELVE

CAPTURED AND RESCUED

☼ARMA☼

Once the girl delivered Kalva's message to the workers in the fields, she felt a great weariness. Her legs ached, and she had a stitch in her side, but worse than those was the feeling that something terrible was about to happen.

Her father had listened, at least. Though Jalo had never paid much attention to his oldest daughter, he did have great respect for Kalva, and her name sent him hurrying among the other family groups in the plantings, warning them to return to the village at once.

Arma pushed her small brothers and sisters toward the village, finding them easier than usual to herd together. Her own fear had caught them, and they fled down the path, leaving her far behind. She turned toward the edge of the trees, searching for more children to move, and found a group of girls sorting turnips into baskets.

"Run to the village!" she called. "Kalva has

warned that there is danger!"

Then she paused, bending to ease the stitch in her side. All about her, people fled past toward the village. She knew that she should run, too, but the pain was too great. At last it loosed its grip, and she straightened.

Even as she did, two men came out of the forest. Tall, pale-haired, they wore deerskin kilts like that the boy had worn. They carried spears, running lightly and easily as if they might run all day without tiring.

She gasped a deep breath and dashed for the path and the distant village. But they were too close, and she had lost too much time. Before she could reach her full speed, they caught up with her, their feet pounding in the soft soil of the field as they neared.

She screamed, but there was nobody left in the field to hear her except for the enemy behind.

She heard an exclamation in a strange tongue, and something struck a savage blow at the back of her head. She fell, face-down, into blackness.

* * * * * * *

At first she thought she was dreaming, but never in her life had she slept hanging head-down, as if lying across a branch. Something warm and firm lay beneath her stomach, and she realized after a moment that she was being carried over a shoulder.

They had knocked her unconscious, and now she was being carried away! She went taut as a bowstring, drawing in her breath to shriek. Before she could cry out, the person who had been carrying her dropped her onto the ground.

She landed so hard that the breath went out of her lungs in a rush, and she found herself gasping for air. By the time she could breathe again, she had calmed a bit, and she looked up, fearing what she might find.

The boy was staring down at her. He had been with those attackers! She opened her mouth again, hoping that someone might hear and come, though she knew that was highly unlikely.

His hand cracked against her cheek. Tears sprang into her eyes, and she put up both hands to ward off another blow. Instead of striking her, he squatted beside her, his face wrinkled with worry. She could see fear in his pale eyes, as they came near her own.

"Ssss!" he hissed. He put his hand over her mouth, then over his own. "Ssss!"

In the distance Arma heard shouts and screams as her people faced attack by his pale companions. Just as Kalva warned, it was happening, and her own kind could spare no time for her, their betrayer.

Tears spilled down her cheeks and fell on her hands as she turned her face toward the boy. Why had he brought her here? What did he intend doing with her? She shivered hard, feeling a sickness rise in her stomach.

He caught her shoulder and shook her hard, his fingers seeming to grip to the bone. Then he loosed his grasp and motioned toward the deeper forest.

Her head ached from the blow, but now her wits were coming back to her. Thinking more clearly, she realized that he might—just might!—not be her enemy, after all. He seemed to want to avoid the attention of any of his fellows in the forest.

And he had given her his beautiful pebble.

What choice did she have? If his people didn't kill her or carry her away as a slave, her own would punish her. The Grandmother, she thought with sudden conviction, would blame her for this entire disaster and would sacrifice her to the Mother Goddess as a traitor. She could not, at this moment, say that would be unjust, but Arma did not want to die.

How had the boy brought her away from the field where she fell? He must, she realized, have waited until his own men had gone on toward the village, for he had not been with them, she was certain. Then...had he come out and taken her away?

She closed her eyes, feeling the salt burn beneath her eyelids. Now her people were being killed. Kalva would need her to prepare herb poultices and to dampen the healing moss....

The boy touched her shoulder again, pointing with his other hand toward the deeper reaches of the wood.

"Kalva!" Arma mourned. "My father and the small ones!"

Although the boy obviously could not understand what she said, he seemed to know what she felt. He patted her shoulder awkwardly and stood, looking down as if assessing what she might be able to do in the forest. Then he reached down and pulled her to her feet.

Never had Arma gone so far among the trees. She stared after the boy, who was moving away without looking back, leaving this decision to her. She knew that he might be leading her away to some terrible torture and death, but he did not go toward the north.

Instead, he angled away toward the stream that, farther down, watered her own village. He was going back! She might learn what happened to her people, if he went on in that direction. For a time, she realized, she must trust this alien stranger.

Moving silently as a breeze over the leaf-strewn floor of the wood, he went toward the stream. She followed, using all the skills she had learned in a lifetime of hunting herbs among the trees, taking care not to crush deadfall underfoot or to push through intertwined bushes instead of bending sideways and sliding between them.

He had tricks of his own, and she imitated his movements as they went. By the time they reached the stream, she was moving almost as silently as the boy.

Slipping into the stream bed, she followed him as he worked his way cautiously toward her village. There, cries were louder, and Arma heard thuds and crackles, as well. The boy paused at last, signaling for her to remain still and silent.

She crept up beside him and peered, through the ferns topping the bank, toward the stockade surrounding the longhouses. Smoke swirled about the village wall, and she could see tongues of flame shooting high above it.

In the green shadow of the stream bed, the boy turned to face her, his expression grim. He pointed toward the pale-haired men who were flinging spears and shooting arrows over the wall into the village. Raising his hand, he spread his fingers, closed his fist, then spread the fingers again.

Five times he did that, and she understood at

last: five hands of warriors had pursued Chass, as he had fled from the northern forest. That many men attacked her people, now, and though her village was a large one, many were children or old people. Of the rest, some were still, she knew, in more distant fields, unaware of the danger to their homes.

She moved until she found a warped pole in the palisade, forming a crack through which she could see into the village. The Mothers' hut was within range of her vision, and she saw flames crackling up from its mud and straw thatch. Some wicked part of her was glad of it, though she tried to quell the blasphemous thought.

As she watched, an attacker squatted beside a pottery jar he had carried and touched the end of a slender torch to the coals inside it. Not a torch—a spear! He tossed the resulting blaze over the wall to strike the top of the nearest of the long houses. That was covered with dirt, luckily, and could not catch fire, but Arma cringed, nevertheless.

The Grandmother stood beside her house, seeming tiny and frail. Yet even from such a distance Arma could feel her anger, burning more hotly than the flames that consumed her home. The old woman was shrieking at the top of her voice, and Arma could hear her words, even above the din of voices inside and the shouts of warriors outside.

"Beasts! Woods-roamers! Forest animals! I curse you! The Mother Goddess will make your flesh rot and your blood burn in your veins!" The words ended in a wail of frustration.

Arma, staring through the crack, could feel the grip of that skinny hand on her arm and could see in her memory the glare of those black eyes. She smiled grimly, knowing that sad as this battle must be, terrible as the suffering it would bring, she was glad to see that old woman brought down.

For the first time in all her life, Arma admitted to herself that she hated and feared the Grandmother, knowing her to be a horrible person. She was cruel to her own people, and she would be much worse to any stranger. She thought that she spoke for the Mother Goddess, but Kalva served the Goddess, too, and she was never cruel.

For the first time, the girl understood why she had dreaded becoming a woman and taking part in the rites the Grandmother and her descendants conducted. Indeed, she thought that any god that one served might well be an enemy of hers.

She glanced aside at the boy. It was plain from his look that he did not want to be seen by any of those who were his own people. He was hiding from them, even as she was, and that was probably the reason why he helped her, upon finding her unconscious in the field.

She wished frantically that they might talk together, for she wanted to know what his situation was. She wished even more deeply that she knew what her own position might be.

He looked up to see her staring at him and quirked an eyebrow, questioning. She nodded, and he moved quietly back upstream to a point at which they could enter the forest unseen.

He led her west and north for a long distance, until her feet were even wearier than before. Her heart was sore, as well, filled with sorrow for her people. Then she began worrying about her own safety.

How did one sleep in the forest without being eaten by the great beasts that prowled the night? What did one eat, besides the roots and herbs and berries that might be in season? She shivered, still following.

A deeper question came to her mind. If she returned to her own village, what might her fate be? Even if the Grandmother should spare her life, and that was more than doubtful, she would force her to mate with the man from Goat Clan. She could not bear that, or to leave Kalva and her work.

Her stomach growled, reminding her of her earlier concern. She had never been away from the village overnight. There alone were safety, shelter, food, and her people. The fields supplied all they needed, though in winter they sometimes had to eat skimpily until the new crops came on again in spring. Fiber plants and goats provided cloth for their clothing. She could not imagine how this boy's people lived, if they did not have such things.

After a long while, the boy paused beside a huge oak tree and looked up into its wide branches. He turned to stare at her, quirking a brow in question.

Arma examined the tree, knowing that he meant for them to sleep high in its branches. They would, she had to admit, be safe there from the dangers that walked the forest floor by night. She sighed and nodded.

He boosted her from behind, until she caught the knack of shinnying up the rough trunk. Climbing high into a complex of branches, she found there was space for them to sit side by side. The tangle of lesser branches would hold them safe, even in their sleep.

She settled into the rough cup as the boy fitted himself in beside her. They said nothing. What would be the point of that, for neither understood the language of the other, more than the few words they had shared.

Arma leaned back, feeling the rough bark cut into her skin. Where would she go from this place? Would she see her family again, or Kalva?

Again, tears filled her eyes, wetting her cheeks as they came. She sobbed quietly, and the boy looked at her, his face dim in the growing dusk. He touched her shoulder with a tentative hand, then put his arm about her.

She was grateful, she found to her surprise, for the warmth of his arm and the comfort of his presence. Then, to her immense surprise, he reached behind and above them and pulled down from some hidden cranny a huge wolf pelt.

It was somewhat stiff and very smelly, but the night air was chilly. She found it wonderfully warm, as, wrapped with the boy in its gray folds, she sank into exhausted sleep.

CHAPTER THIRTEEN

TEARING THE HEART

☼BAIN☼

Kesh ran toward the tribal village, his pace already gaining speed with his warning. Bain, high in a tree and hidden among the leaves like an overlarge squirrel, knew the sharp-eyed hunter too well to risk even a peep. A hunter felt, he knew, when he was being looked at.

Kesh would know instantly if anyone spied upon him as he ran, though there had been no sign that any of the group suspected they might be watched. Only when the hunter's running steps had gone beyond hearing did the boy come down the tree.

What would be best to do? He could allow these strangers to surprise his own people without warning, but that was no longer a danger. Now he felt suddenly responsible for those distant and unsuspecting villagers.

Was it possible that he might outrun the hunters now following those behind him? Might he reach the village ahead of them and the warriors who would be sent on by the shaman, in order to warn the girl in time? He knew that he must try, even if he arrived too late.

He retrieved his wolf-pelt and his cloak, tying them firmly to his back. He had earned that skin, no matter if it slowed him a bit, and he had no intention of losing it.

Then he set out at an easy trot through the forest, avoiding the track that his people had followed. Angling away from their route, he took a direct one, for he had calculated his directions closely as he left the village. He could, he thought, take much shorter ways and arrive before the hunters.

In the days he had traveled before, he had taken his time. Killing the wolf and treating the hide had taken days, but now he had no intention of pausing except occasionally for food and at night for safe sleep. He would arrive at his destination, he felt, at least as soon as those dark-haired men who had followed him.

He arrived at the oak in which he had slept while near the village in just half the time it had taken him to travel home again. He climbed high in the tree and fixed his wolf skin into a crotch above a platform made of several large branches that sprang outward to form his old sleeping place.

Relieved of his burden, he moved down again to find a frugal supper of grasshoppers, grubs, and berries. After that, in the twilight, he crept near the village to check, but there was no sign that anything was amiss. It would be morning before the girl might come to the wood.

He would rest in safety from his hurried journey, and tomorrow he would keep watch for her. He would find some way to warn her of the approaching danger from the north. He could detect no sign of the men who had pursued him northward, and he hoped he was in good time to prevent a disaster.

He woke with first light, and by full day he was near the village, again high in a tree. From its top, he could look over the wall into the village, and in the other direction he could see into the fields. The girl was not visible, either in the village or coming toward the forest.

When he saw her, at last, she was bending over a pot that stood beside the fire in front of a squat hut standing at the farther side of the enclosure. She added hot stones from the coals, from time to time, to keep the pot boiling—his people did just the same, and he supposed that she was cooking.

As he watched, the sun rose higher and the girl continued her work. Bain settled comfortably into his tree, for until she came into the wood he could not try to warn her.

* * * * * * *

The time passed very slowly. Bain was almost dozing when he heard the sound of heavy feet trampling through the wood off to the east of his position. They would pass at some distance, he knew, but he lay flat on one of the thick branches, blotting out his human outline from any observant eye.

Once they had gone, he raised his head and looked toward the path leading to the village. There were the three he had seen, he was almost sure, in the forest far to the north. They ran fast, and he knew that they fled from warriors of the People, sent after them by the Shaman.

He moved closer and climbed another tree to watch as they staggered into the walled enclosure and two of them fell, exhausted, to the ground. The third ran to a hut, much larger than the one where the girl was working, that stood close inside the gate.

Bain shivered. He knew his own people were close, now, and time grew short. Kesh would have run like the wind to bring a party to join the others, and the entire group must now be very near. They were great hunters, and their skills at war, in occasional skirmishes with other hunting tribes, were sound.

In their ears he knew that they still heard the waspish voice of the Shaman as he sent them to kill those who intruded into their hunting grounds. "Kill them!" he would have said, as he had heard him say about his own kind, at times, when someone questioned orders.

As he watched the village, he saw the girl leave her pot at last and come running toward the field near the stream. He understood at once that she had been sent to warn the people working there, and indeed in a short time everyone was hurrying back toward the safety of the walls.

He turned to look down into the forest behind his tree, and there he saw pale gleams that were the heads of his own kind. Three headed straight toward the field where she stood, bent oddly instead of running. They would catch her!

He slid from the tree, barking his knees and elbows, and ran toward her. Reaching the bed of the stream, he dropped into its shelter and followed it toward the spot where the girl had been. The covert would hide him from his own people, as well as from any of hers who might still be outside the village.

Once he drew even with the field, he rose and peered between the fern stalks. The field seemed empty at first, but at the farther edge he realized that men were moving toward the village. Those were the ones he saw from the treetop. Where was she?

He climbed up the bank and once he was upright he saw a crumpled shape lying in the dust of the field. Glancing nervously toward the forest and toward the village, he found to his relief that no one was in sight. Then he hurried to her side and dropped to his knees.

It was the right girl. He had known that, in some way, all the while.

He caught her by the shoulders and dragged her into the shelter of the stream, where he managed to get her limp body across his shoulder. She was smaller than he, not nearly as heavy, but it was with some difficulty that he carried her upstream and then away into the wood.

He struggled on for a long while, afraid to stop until he was well clear of any route the warriors might explore. He knew she was alive, for her heart thudded against his shoulder, but was she badly hurt? There had been a lump on her head, but he had no time to check for other damage.

Her breathing had been steady for a long while, when she went suddenly tense against his arm and shoulder. He felt the intake of breath that told him she was about to shout, and he dropped her, hard, flat on the ground.

He felt both relieved and angry. Didn't she know he had been trying to save her? She glared up at him, and her mouth opened again. He had to stop that, though he guessed how frightened she must be. They couldn't risk rousing the attention of anyone in the wood.

If only he could talk with her! He hated slapping her, but once she calmed a bit he did the best he could to make her understand their danger. Even as he did, he wondered if she was capable of moving cautiously and quietly enough to follow him down-stream and check on her people. If his own family had been involved in a battle, he would want to know how they fared.

It took a bit of work, but at last he was satisfied that she understood him. As they moved toward the stream again, he noted that she stepped quietly and followed his example.

Once they came within sight of the village, he was sickened to see the fire and the flying arrows. He was watching one of his own people lighting a fire-spear when the man, feeling his gaze on his back, turned and stared into the reeds and ferns.

Bain sank back and lay very still. Only when the man returned to his duty did the boy lead the girl back toward the forest and safety.

They must reach the tree in which he had left his wolf skin. Nights were growing very cool, and they needed its warmth. Once they were in the cup of branches, wrapped in the skin, he found that the girl seemed glad of it, stink though it might.

She did not cry again. Not while she was awake. But he felt her sobbing in her sleep and tightened the arm about her shoulders. Even he had felt shaken to see her people being attacked, and it must be far worse if they were your own.

As he dozed beside her warm shape, he felt that he understood many things he had never known before. Hunting beasts was dangerous work, and you went with care and prayer to the Horned God. Men were far more dangerous, and no amount of prayer would protect you from their onslaughts, when there was anger in them.

He found that he wanted to cry, himself, but he settled instead against the girl, warm in the wolf skin, and closed his eyes. Tomorrow would bring decisions he didn't like to think about. But rest and, later, food must come before anything else.

CHAPTER FOURTEEN

THE WORLD HAS CHANGED

☼BAIN☼

Bain woke when the sky paled beyond the eastern treetops, feeling the touch of frost that nipped in the air. Fall was here, and winter would be coming soon, driving him into some sort of shelter, wherever he could find it.

He had turned in his sleep, and the girl was huddled against his back, warm and companionable. The wolf skin held their combined heat in its odorous folds, but his knees had been outward and were chilled. He pulled them up against his stomach, hating to expose himself to this new and unpredictable day.

Within the past weeks his entire world had changed completely from the one he had known all his life. His father was gone, and his mother was as lost to him as if she, too, had died. He had now seen other people than the hunting tribes and spoken words that were not in his own tongue.

Worst of all, he knew that the Shaman was his

bitter enemy and would put him to death if he were caught in the northern forest again. He could never return to his kin and must wander until he found another clan, another family who would accept him into its security.

Now he had seen, as well as heard of, men killing men without a blood feud to give them reason. The sort of madness he had seen the day before made him feel sick and dizzy.

He shivered, thinking of it, remembering the still shapes he had seen inside the wall. Two of his own people had lain dead before the wall, as well, with short spears studding their bodies.

He clenched his teeth, thinking that the Shaman was sitting in his double-thick tent in the forest, safe and comfortable after having caused all this suffering. For generations he and his fathers had sacrificed great hunters every seven years, claiming that their deaths enriched the forest, making game plentiful. Now Bain had seen other places and other ways, and he was becoming certain that the Horned God could not be controlled by an old man without teeth who ordered his own people killed.

Indeed, Bain had seen the great beast himself, and his steps had followed the god's guidance.

No, the Shaman had used the god as a justification and a lever for his own power, dominating his people for as long as he could remember. Men and women and children had died at a whim, even outside the cycle of sacrifice to the god, and no one had dared to protest.

Now, lying snug against the girl, he remembered every person he knew who had, in one way or another, run afoul of the Shaman, by questioning commands or looking as if they disagreed, even if they said nothing. All had died of illness, he knew, but he also knew his mother's warnings against certain plants that grew in the forest. Poison, he now thought, might well have carried out the old man's revenge for real or imagined wrongs.

Opening his eyes again to see the slow fingering of sunlight among the leaves above him, he knew that even if he could, he would not go back to live beneath that domineering eye. He could no more go back to being the Bain he had been than a hawk could return to the egg.

What of the girl? Would she go back, when the fighting was over, to her people? She would, he knew, for there was no reason why she should remain in the wood just to keep him from being lonely.

The forest was endless to the north, and he had seen for great distances into the grasslands beyond the village. They, too, seemed to have no end, though they were sometimes broken by small groves. He would drift like a feather on a stream through this boundless world, with no root and no friend.

The thought made him feel cold and forsaken.

The girl stirred and stretched, and he turned to face her as she pushed back the fur and sat. She wrinkled her nose with distaste as she caught a gust of stink from the hide, but she seemed to have cried herself out in the night. Her face was marked with tears, and her eyes were round, but as much with curiosity, he thought, as with fear.

Bain laid his hand on the folds of the wolf pelt and said, "Wolf," very distinctly. He watched her

97

for some reaction.

She laid her hand beside his and riffled the fur between her fingers. "Wolf?" she asked.

He made tracks in the coarse hair with his nails, saying, "Fur."

She smoothed out his marks and made others of her own. "Fur."

Sitting there, their hungry bellies growling, they named the trees, the squirrels, which were going about their morning business vigorously, and the deer that moved below in the wood. Bain named his arms and legs and hair and nose, though he could think of no way to indicate "go" or "hungry" or any words that might help them talk over what they should do next. Yet they were beginning to understand each other just a bit, and that was good.

The girl solved some of his problem by pointing to her mouth and then to her stomach. "Food," she said. "Eat." She made chewing motions, and he understood at once.

So that was the way to go about it. Taking a hint from her, he pointed down at the ground beneath the tree.

"Go," he said. "Go."

CHAPTER FIFTEEN

DECISIONS

ARMA

Arma felt, she was sure, like one of the roots she had so often pulled from the ground and put into her string bag. She had been uprooted and carried away from everything familiar.

Once she was wide awake and had gathered her wits, she drew away from the boy's warm side, still seeing those pale-haired men burning her village and killing her people with spears and arrows. But she knew that this boy had saved her life, very probably.

If the men who had struck her had returned to find her helpless, she would have died or been enslaved, and one was as bad as the other. Those warriors would not have been tender with her, she knew. Yet the thought of her family and of Kalva was a pain inside as she turned to the boy.

He seemed, strangely enough, to understand. His word-game distracted her thoughts from more painful things, and she began to feel real interest as they exchanged terms for all the things within range of their busy eyes.

After some time, she began to know how empty her stomach was, how dirty and itchy her skin and face. She tried combing her tangled hair with her fingers, but it was filled with dust from the field. When he signaled that they should go down, she was more than ready.

He led her surely to a stream, a tiny trickle gushing from beneath a stone to fall into a fern-lined pool. She squatted beside the boy and cupped her hands to drink. Once both had drunk their fill, she plunged her head beneath the water.

Cold as it was, she was brought tinglingly awake, and she slipped off her apron and moved to sit in the pool, scrubbing her skin and hair with hands and sand from the bank. The boy plunged into a larger pool downstream, and he also washed well. Handfuls of ferns helped to remove the excess water, once the pair climbed out onto the grass.

Shivering, they put on apron and kilt again, but the contrast between the skin that had been covered was marked. Beneath her apron, she was a smooth golden brown, only slightly paler than her arms and face. But his skin untouched by sun was strangely colorless.

She pointed to his hip and said, "White." Then she pointed to her own. "Brown."

He nodded, but she knew by his eyes that he was thinking again of more important matters. She sighed, allowing her mind to return to the problems the two of them faced.

Where would they go? How would they live? She had seen that he avoided his own kind, and that told her he could not or would not go back with them when they went north again. She wondered what she would do, for that matter, for going back into the hands of the Grandmother was a thing she dreaded.

If the village survived, what sort of life could she find there? She knew that the Mothers would not allow her to help Kalva for long. They would, if she were not blamed for bringing the attack down on her people, force her to marry Levan of the Goat Clan.

Once she was trapped into the life of a woman of the tribe, she would never again have the opportunity to learn the things Kalva was teaching her. The skills she had learned as an herbalist would be wasted, for that was a demanding art.

She should continually try new plants for usefulness or toxicity, testing out mixtures and tinctures and teas. There was always sickness or childbirth or injury needing the skills of a healer, and one who was busy with digging in the fields or working at making cloth or tending infants had no time to sharpen her skills.

Her own family was no longer hers. Roma was the mother there now, and Kiri would run to her, not to her sister. Her father was silent and undemonstrative, and he seemed not to miss having her about.

Most of all, she did not want to see the Grandmother again, not ever. Her faith in the wisdom of the Three had been shattered, for it was the Grandmother's decision to send runners after the boy that had brought this catastrophe down upon her people.

Let her blame Arma as she would, the old woman must know that. And if her judgment was faulty, how could that of the Mother Goddess be any better?

Arma found now that she had never held the same awe of the goddess that her mother and the other women seemed to have. The rituals that were a part of village life seemed dull and time-wasting to her, and those others that were open only to women had filled her with dread, from the time she learned something about them. No, she could not return to that.

The boy touched her shoulder and pointed. "Go?"

He was gesturing toward the village, and she found herself drawn, against her will, toward her people's dwellings. If nothing else, she must spy to see who had survived, and she wanted to find a chance to speak to Kalva again.

Nodding, she fastened her apron behind her.

The boy's smile was rather sad, as he laid his hand over his heart. "Bain," he said.

"Oh." She had not found the time to wonder about his name. "Arma," she said, laying her own hand over her heart. Something warmed inside her. Once more they had exchanged gifts.

He finished tying his kilt and headed toward the stream, and she followed him, silent but thinking hard. She didn't want to rejoin her people, for she now saw the possibility of choices she had never had before. She was not condemned to live in the village.

She went after Bain into a thicket soaked with the drizzle that had begun as low clouds came in from the west. Finding the stream, they crept along its shelter, the cold water chilling their ankles, until they came level with the village.

Arma could see that a section of the palisade was down, the heavy logs still smoldering. The hut where the Mothers had lived was a pile of ash, with drifts of smoke still drifting up into the damp air.

She stared anxiously toward Kalva's hut, and to her relief it was standing, though the fire in front of the doorway had gone out. People were moving about in the village, some limping, most looking dazed.

She almost ran out to help, for she could see burns and wounds soaking through the bandages of moss, but she held herself back. That might be very dangerous, both for her and for her companion.

As Arma watched, her father came out of the long house. Kiri came behind him, and they both seemed unhurt. If one of the family had died, surely neither would look so cheerful, she thought.

Then the Grandmother came out of Kalva's tiny hut, followed by her daughter and granddaughter, though Arma wondered how the three could possibly crowd into that small space. The old woman raised a hand, and Chass, who had run up to her as she emerged, went into the small house where wood was stored out of the wet.

After a long moment, he came out again, his hands busy controlling the struggling figure of the herb woman. Kalva was kicking at his legs, but he was too tall for her, and her feet waved uselessly above the ground.

"Kalva!" shrieked the girl, rising from the stream and running toward the fallen wall. Only when she was inside did she realize that Bain had not followed her.

She didn't blame him, and if she could have un-done her rash action she would have. But it was too late, and she knew she must live with the consequences.

Two young men from Dog Clan were holding Kalva. The Grandmother, who had begun to speak, paused to see what this interruption might be, and once Arma stood before her the old woman's eyes began glittering wickedly.

"So you are not dead or carried away as a captive. It was you...."—she nodded for the men to release Kalva—"who first saw that pale-haired boy. Kalva brought the word to me, but you gave it to her. I should have remembered that. You are the one who must suffer for bringing death and destruction upon your people!"

Arma found to her surprise that she was not frightened of the Grandmother now. She pulled herself as straight and tall as she could before saying, "I saw what was there to be seen. I told Kalva, as duty demanded. If you think that I caused this, you cannot be wise."

She stared into those black snake eyes, feeling a rush of anger. "You are only a foolish old woman, fit for nothing but tending fires and sharpening sticks!"

Once the words were out beyond recall, Arma was appalled. Why had she dared to speak in that way to the holy woman of her people? And yet she was not ashamed, though the people standing about them in a wide circle were gasping with shock.

She could not be in worse trouble now, no matter what she might say, so she went on recklessly. "You sent Chass and Urlo and Greb after that boy, and that was what brought those warriors down upon us. You wanted to sacrifice him to the Mother Goddess, and you took no thought to what the result might be. You should offer yourself to her, if any-one is to die!"

Urlo leaped upon her, with Levan from the Goat Clan. They dragged her arms behind her to be tied fast, but she glared at the old woman still, without regret that she had spoken her thoughts without fear.

"Put her in the hut. Tie her securely." The Grandmother's voice was thin with fury. "We shall have a sacrifice fit for the Mother Goddess...a woman of childbearing age has never been sent to Her. A blasphemer is a suitable gift to secure us from further attack."

She did not pause in her ranting, as Arma was dragged to Kalva's hut. The worktable and bench had been stripped out, leaving the floor clear, and onto that Urlo pushed her, tying her to the center post that held up the roof. Then he and Levan tied a screen of wattles across the door.

She could hear the talk outside clearly, as Kalva's voice sounded in the sudden quiet when the Grandmother paused for breath. "You have thrown my medicines out into the rain, though they are needed to heal our sick and wounded. You threaten to kill me, though I am the only healer you have.

"Now you propose to sacrifice my only suitable apprentice. The madness of the moon has seized you, Elna, daughter of Otha."

Arma grinned. Kalva might be foolish to risk herself by standing up for her apprentice, but no-body had ever doubted her courage.

Kalva had known the Grandmother for longer

than anyone else in the tribe, being only a little younger than she. To call the Grandmother by her Earth-Name was both a personal insult and a denial of her right to call herself priestess of the Mother Goddess. Arma shivered to think how the healer might suffer for that.

There came a hubbub, and then the village was strangely silent. Arma guessed that the men had again imprisoned Kalva for further discussion of her fate. She sagged against the roof-pole, suddenly drained of energy.

Night seemed to take forever to arrive, for she had been captured very early. Nobody came near her, and Arma grew thirsty and hungry. The tight cords binding her to the pole hurt her wrists and her legs, and she felt sick and light-headed.

When at last it was fully dark, she listened hard to hear if a guard had been set outside her hut. She heard nothing, not a breath or a cough or the creak of the wicker wall, where someone might lean against it to rest.

They had probably set their sentinels outside the wall or in the edge of the forest, on watch for the return of their attackers. No one had asked how she escaped or if she had anyone with her, and she knew they thought that she had hidden during the fighting and returned only when it was safe.

If she managed to wriggle loose from her bindings, she thought she might find a way out of the hut and through the wall away from the forest. She might even find Bain, who seemed her only hope of escape from this place that would mean her death if she stayed.

Backing against the pole, she began scrubbing

her bound wrists against the rough bark, up and down, up and down. The rubbing wore away as much skin as it did the grass cord, she thought. Trickles of blood ran warm down her wrists, but she kept at it persistently.

In the total darkness, she could feel occasional drips of rain fall through the roof onto her neck and back. The rain was a good thing. It might well cover her escape, if she managed to get free, though the cord was proving tougher than she had thought.

She had, she realized, been hearing a soft sound beyond the wall for some time before she really was conscious of it. Something worked quietly at the wattle screen covering the door, and she could hear the sound of breath in the darkness.

"Kalva?" she whispered.

"Bain." The word was the merest breath, but it told her that the boy had not left her to her fate. He must have watched the village until it was safe to creep into the compound (and how had he managed that?) to free her.

She felt a surge of warmth in her chilled heart. She did have a friend, no matter that her world had crumbled about her head. Bain and Kalva could be depended on, of all the people she knew.

The wattle gave with a soft creak, and she heard him enter the hut. A touch at her wrist told her he was fumbling with the cords, and soon they fell away. She moved her hands, trying to work the circulation back into her fingers, while Bain waited patiently.

He led her out, crawling flat and moving by digging in with elbows and knees. The rain had made the dust of the village compound into mud, which while nasty was also quiet. Instead of heading for the gate or the burned portion of the wall, Bain led off to the south wall.

The Grandmother had set no sentinels there, expecting attack only from the north and east. That seemed foolish, but Arma was glad of it.

They crept through a cranny between two crooked logs and found themselves outside the wall. Making a long curve behind the village, they moved back to the forest.

Arma was exhausted, wet and muddy and chilled to the bone. Her head and hands and muscles ached, and she was weak, for she had eaten nothing all day.

It would be morning before they could find food, she knew, but she also understood that she must explain to Bain, in some way yet to be found, why she must risk another trip to the village. She could not let Kalva suffer.

She would find and free the healer, for Arma knew that when the Grandmother found her first victim gone she would replace her with Kalva. Her insult had been a mortal one, impossible to forget or ignore.

Rescuing her teacher would not be easy. They would have to wait out the day until darkness fell again. Arma must creep through the compound from their convenient crack, trying to find the place where the old woman was held. Bain must not come, for if she were caught he would need to try rescuing her once more.

Warm in the wolf skin at last, she sighed and snuggled against the boy's back. He would understand, she hoped, when she tried to explain her plan.

And if he did not—she would go alone.

CHAPTER SIXTEEN

ANOTHER RESCUE

BAIN

Bain opened his eyes to the new day, feeling stiff and achy. Even the wolf skin had not kept off all the damp from the rain, which fell steadily in the night. Though the tree protected them to some extent, his hair was beaded with wet, dripping as he groaned and sat.

Beside him, the girl stirred and sat too, blinking away tears of rain. He tried to grin at her, but he was too hungry and cold to make a good job of it.

Arma seemed to understand, for she grimaced as she stretched. Then she reached to touch his hand, leaning close as if that would help her to make him understand her words.

"Bain, I...."—she pointed to herself to make the point—"must go back." She pointed to the village and looked very sad. "Kalva is there. She is tied as I was." Here she crossed her wrists and showed him the raw welts left by the cords that had bound her. "Kalva. My friend. Do you understand?"

Although it was the gestures more than the words that told him what she meant, he nodded, knowing her concern. It had been the sight of the old woman being dragged out of the house that had set the girl off. And afterward he had seen the woman bundled into a low shed that seemed to hold firewood. Was she Arma's grandmother? He had no way to know.

But he would help his own family, if he could. Indeed, he had put his life in danger because he refused to injure his father! Yet here there was a very cold, clear danger, for they had gone to the village already. Surely the villagers would guard against their return.

They must certainly be keeping close eyes upon the wood and the stream. He had seen beyond any doubt that they were not friendly to Arma, for she had been bound after she ran to help the old woman. Was she facing such a fate as the Shaman meant for him, there in her own home?

"Too risky," he said in his own tongue, but he shook his head so she would understand.

The girl shook the damp from her hair and bound it into a tight braid with quick fingers. "I will go alone," she said. He knew go. Alone he did not understand, but from the look in her eyes he caught the meaning.

He thought of being alone in the forest over the coming winter, with no companion at his side. He sighed, and then he nodded.

They washed again, for the rain was too light to do anything except make them feel greasily damp. Bain was also hungry, and he pointed to his mouth, then to his stomach.

"Food. Eat," he said.

She nodded vigorously.

He had made do with grubs and berries for too long. Now he needed a fat hare or a couple of squirrels. His sling was, as always, in the loop beneath his kilt, and he found plenty of pebbles in the bottom of the brook. Taking a handful, he crammed them into his pouch.

Arma followed him into the trees, but he stopped her with a gesture and sent her climbing into a nearby tree. She must remain silent and out of sight, for stalking small game was best done alone, by an expert.

The fall morning was alive with small scutterings among the dead leaves and brush. Wet though it was, they must feed, and he caught glimpses of gray fur and brown, as he crept through the wood. Lying flat in a ferny spot, he watched the hares hopping along their tiny trails, choosing a large young animal as his quarry.

But as he moved gently to make his cast, something else caught his eye. Beyond the beech tree in which squirrels were playing, a large, fat hare was nibbling grass in the early morning light.

Changing his aim, he followed through with his cast, and the hare rolled over, kicking, and then lay still. Bain sighed, hearing the squirrels still playing high in the beech tree. He had been lucky, this morning, and so had the squirrels. A single large hare provided more food than several squirrels.

When he returned and called Arma down from her perch, she came gladly. He used his flint knife to gut the hare, saving the skin and stretching it for later scraping. The girl grimaced when he handed her a bloody haunch of the animal, but she chewed resolutely, and he knew she understood why they could not risk a fire.

No matter which of their peoples came to investigate a smoke, one of them would be in trouble. They had to remain hidden, secret, if they were to free that old woman in the village.

When they were full of hare, and Arma had added some roots she grubbed up beside the brook, Bain felt much better about their expedition. They washed the blood from their hands and faces, and then he moved toward the stream that afforded the best and most concealed approach to the village. But this time, as they crept down, knee deep in the water in the shelter of the banks, he heard a sigh and the shifting of feet around the bend ahead.

This time the stream bed was guarded. He could smell the smoky odor on the skins of the men waiting there, and he could hear their noisy movements as they hid. Arma had sprung up from this stream to run toward the village, the day before. That must have warned them that it was a route for danger.

The villagers should, he thought with wry amusement, have thought of that sooner. It was easy to see that they were not used either to hunting or war, for any hunter was infinitely superior to these farmers in that skill.

He almost laughed. There were any number of directions leading to that village. While waiting to free Arma, he had ranged around the place, keeping hidden without difficulty from the unwary watchers.

To the south, between the wall and the fields, there lay a wide tumble of scrub bushes and rocks. The ground there was poor, overgrown with thickets of thorn and bramble that grew to the height of a tall man. It was a perfect place for hiding, and from it the pair of them could launch their effort to free Kalva.

He slid back upstream and into the forest, with Arma coming behind so quietly that he had to halt often to see that she was still with him. In that she was better than the women of the People, for they tended to chatter, even when that was dangerous.

The sun was almost overhead before they circled widely and reached the spot he had chosen. They went slowly and with much caution, for he felt that Kesh might have left some of his people to keep watch on the village, in case these people chose to pursue their attackers. He had no wish to stumble on such a sentry.

He didn't think of stopping for more food. They had eaten well, and not until their bellies growled and there was a proper time and place for hunting would they stop again to eat. That was the way of his people; hunger was a thing to be ignored.

They came to the edge of the rough ground, which extended some distance into the thinly wooded hem of the forest. Broken stone thrust up between tree roots for some way before he came to the spot he had pinpointed. There scrub grew right up to the palisade, which was not intelligent from a defensive viewpoint. The fence was built to keep out large animals, not men, it was plain.

He guided Arma into the shelter of a thick clump of bushes, most of them still well leafed, though the leaves were browning at the edges. This kept out the worst of the drizzle, and he buried the two of them in the fallen leaves of past years. They dozed and watched as the day wore on with dreadful slowness.

When twilight covered the land, Bain stirred and pushed aside the layer of leaves covering them as they lay in a hollow among the roots. He lifted himself on his hands and stared toward the wall of the village, now a blur in the wet gloom.

He looked back at Arma. "I go," he said softly.

Arma crept beside him as he moved through the thicket of briar and thorn and wild fruit trees. By the time they reached his chosen section of the south wall, it was fully dark. Fires burned in the doors of the longhouses, though after a time hide coverings were pulled over them to keep out the autumn chill.

He lay beside the girl; both were flat on their stomachs in a grassy spot, damp but more comfortable than roots and rocks. The drizzle stopped in a bit, and the cloud layer moved off to the west, leaving the moon to show through as a bright patch above the eastern forest.

One by one, the fires were quenched, covered with ash to hold the coals until morning. Except for occasional wails from infants, the compound was silent.

CHAPTER SEVENTEEN

RESCUING KALVA

☼BAIN☼

The moon, rising above the haze of cloud, gave just enough light to make everything inside the compound either black or some shade of gray. Bain knew where the old woman had been confined; he could go directly to the shed. He started forward, but Arma caught his shoulder.

"I go," she said.

He sank onto his haunches and strained to see her face. "No. I see...."—he pointed to his eyes—"old woman...."—he hunched over to look as old and feeble as possible—"put there." He pointed to the gray-barred pole structure.

"Oh." She nodded, and he knew she understood what he had said. She had been in the hut, shut away, but now he knew she realized that he could see what happened, as she had not been able to.

She sank into cover and nodded. He crept forward to the wall and fumbled to find the crack, where there was a loose log. He tugged at it, tumbling it outward, toward him. They could push it back into place, once he returned, and no one would know it had been moved. They could creep through the crack, but the old woman was entirely too large, and this space would give her room to pass.

Once he had cleared the way, he turned to wave at Arma, though he could not see her. Then he slid inside and sank onto his belly, listening for any movement. He slipped like a snake through the mud and trampled grass of the compound, keeping to uneven patches of ground for cover. He took advantage of every shadow and hummock, and soon he was beside the pole hut.

He lay beside its wall, listening for movement inside. At last he could detect light, controlled breathing and knew that she was listening to the night as intently as he.

"Kalva," he whispered between two poles. "Arma...." Then he stopped, finding nothing more that she would understand.

But the two names were enough. There came a sharp "Ssss!" from inside the shed. "I will go with you," she said.

He only understood go, but that was enough. He pulled at the grass rope that held the poles securing the door of thc shed. When they went slack, he cut the rest with his flint knife. The old woman thrust her bound wrists out and bumped his side, and he cut those cords, too.

He had expected her to be stiff with long inaction, and she was. Even a young person could not remain bound for so long without feeling the effect of it, and she was very old. Her bones and muscles should have weakened and become fragile, yet she crawled out of the shed on hands and knees and followed him across the compound toward the wall without any complaint.

As they reached the wall, there came the sound of voices at the gate on the other side of the village. The sentinels were being changed, and their two dark shapes against the frost-pale grass might be visible.

Something whizzed over Bain's back and thudded into the side of a house. The crack sounded loudly in the still night. Another hit Kalva's hut, and the men at the gate ran toward the house, yelling, confused.

Bain and Kalva scooted through the gap in the wall and pushed the log back into place, propping the section with a stone. Then they dived into the tangle of growth, moving deeper and deeper without raising their heads, until they burrowed into the scrub beside Arma.

Beyond the wall there was a babble of noise. Torches flared, lighting the chinks between the logs, and they could catch glimpses of searchers combing the compound. They focused their hunt about the longhouse and Kalva's hut. They searched the pole structure as well, and the discovery of her escape roused even more confusion.

Bain reached to touch Arma's hand, giving it a quick squeeze. She had seen the danger and had acted instantly to help. It would not occur to anyone to search outside the walls for some time, and even then there was no reason to believe searchers would come in this direction.

He led the pair back into the wood west of the village, making false turns and covering their disturbance of the low-growing branches as well as he could. The moon was going down in the west by the time they reached the forest.

Kalva, for all her determination, was exhausted. She had lain for a night and a day in a damp shed, tied and helpless, without food or water. It was wonderful to him that she moved at all, and the deep cough that now shook her troubled Bain. She must have warmth and food, though food must wait until morning.

He put his shoulder under one of the old woman's arms, and Arma took her other side. Half carrying her, they struggled through the wood, though Bain knew too well how dangerous that might prove in the darkness.

A big cat made its kill some distance to the west, and out in the grasslands a wolf pack was in full cry after some unlucky prey. Ahead a she-bear grunted, but she was a long way away.

They came at last to his tree, though it was terribly hard getting Kalva up into it. She put forth all the strength left in her tough old body, however, and aided by both of them she went up at last. Once she reached the first branches, which were wide and not too far apart, she managed better, though she groaned with effort and pain.

Once they were settled together, rather crowded but safe, in the cup of branches, Bain brought down the wolf skin from the fork where he kept it by day. Once they had huddled together tightly, wrapped in the smelly folds, Kalva relaxed.

Bain's rump was near the edge of the hide, and he suspected that Arma's was getting a draught on the other, but the skin almost completely covered them all. Kalva was warm, and that was enough.

Though the moon was all but down, they could see each other's faces above the edge of the hide, dappled with the shadows of leaves. Kalva and Arma began talking in low voices, but Bain was too tired to strain to hear the few words he knew.

After a time, the woman turned her sharp gaze upon him, and he looked into her eyes. They reminded him of the Shaman's, though where his were angry and held a hint of cruelty, this old woman's were merely bright and intelligent.

She smiled at last and patted his shoulder. "Well done, Bain," she said.

He smiled, hearing his name. Her voice was comforting, deep and gentle like his mother's. He understood why Arma had been willing to risk recapture to save her. She was truly a wise woman, not like the Shaman or that angry old woman in her village. Such a wise elder was one that every tribe must have, if it was to prosper.

Arma reached across the healer to take his hand. "Thank you, Bain," she said.

He needed no translation for her words.

CHAPTER EIGHTEEN

A NEW DIRECTION

☼ARMA☼

Arma felt as if she had been swept away by a windstorm or a flood. Suddenly, unexpectedly, she was free of the demands of the Grandmother and her own family. She had no responsibility for any sickness in her village, no duties to fulfill, no fear of Levan of the Goat Clan.

The past days seemed like a dream, rushing by her so swiftly that she had only quick images left in her memory. Her life had always been the same, since she was a child, for few changes were allowed by the Mothers. Such a drastic thing as the one she had just witnessed left her dizzy.

She had longed to follow Bain into the forest, and here she was, where she wanted to be. It was as if the Mother Goddess, weary of the manipulations of the Grandmother, had reached down and taken this child of hers out of the reach of the old woman's long arm. Even better, Kalva was with her, too. That made her feel that, though she was cast adrift from her roots, she was not totally bereft of everything familiar and secure.

Bain, new friend though he was, already was a reassuring presence. He knew the ways of the forest, while her people did not. If she must live there, it was best to have someone at her side who knew how to hide and to hunt. Let the Grandmother fret and call down curses upon her as she might, Arma knew she preferred the new and unknown future to that one she had dreaded for so long.

She had lived for some time as if working in her sleep, accepting what came. This was the way the Grandmother had taught her tribe to live. Now it was easier, Arma found, to drift after Bain than to worry. Change was all about her, but for the time being she needed to adjust to it.

* * * * * * *

As soon as Kalva could travel, Bain led them deeper into the forest north of the village. They could not risk fire, and though he returned with fat hares and skinny squirrels, they had to eat them raw and bloody, and Arma soon wearied of that.

Of course the Grandmother sent out searchers after her and Kalva, and for several days Arma huddled high in their sturdy tree with her companions. They could not risk going down to hunt by day, and it was too dangerous by night.

Luckily, those from the village never thought to look up into the treetops, and the fugitives remained unseen, though they were very hungry. Occasional rain helped, for they could lick it from the tree bark and squeeze it from the rank hairs of the wolf skin.

Never would the girl have thought she could savor water the color of mud, tasting of dead wolf, but it quenched her thirst, and that was enough.

Once they were able to leave the vicinity of the village, Arma began to learn the very different skills that she was going to need. She was now glad that her own kind had lacked them, for if they had possessed them it meant they might have recaptured the runaways, to be sacrificed to the goddess.

They traveled for days, moving slowly, for trying to hurry made Kalva cough deeply. At last the old woman healed enough to allow them to make haste. Once they were well away from danger Bain returned to hunting.

They lacked a pot for boiling his small game, but a spit over their fire substituted very well. Never had cooked meat tasted so fine, Arma thought.

At night, tucked high in a tree that had enough branches to let Kalva climb it, they exchanged words in both languages, and by the time the moon was new again they all understood a usable amount of both tongues.

That allowed Bain to explain why he needed to take them so far from both their village and his own. Only distance, he explained with words and signs and drawings in the dirt, would give them any security.

He also suggested finding a spot for a permanent camp. It was clear that Kalva could not continue walking through the forest in winter. She would die, and Arma knew that her death would leave the two younger people the poorer. With a healer to care for them, they might survive...even form, in time, the beginning of a new family. Without her they were likely to die of sickness or injury, far from any source of help.

Arma knew that in time she and Bain would choose to be mates. With Kalva to guide them, the rituals would be done correctly, according to the ancient teachings of the people. Having a healer would be vital when children were born or bones were broken or sickness plagued them.

A rest camp was necessary for them all, so Arma searched with the others until they found, at last, a cave cut into the side of a hill by a stream. The water lay far below the lip of the opening, having worn through the rock until it made a great cut across the forest.

The cave was deep enough for shelter, though they all knew it was not large enough to spend a winter. There was no room to store provisions and firewood. Yet they could pause here and rest and make plans for the future.

She waited there with Kalva, weaving rushes and willow withes into baskets, while Bain snared small game and hunted with his bow for deer, whose hides would make winter clothing. Cold winds already swept down from the north, bringing volleys of dead leaves from the trees, and they all shivered in their light garments.

Bain was either a lucky hunter or a very good one, she decided, when he began bringing gutted deer and badger and even an otter or two to the cave. She skinned them out carefully, first at his direction and then on her own. Kalva understood how to treat skins, too, and between them they scraped and pounded and dried and stretched furs and hides.

Kalva punched holes and cut shapes with Bain's

flint knife and laced them together into leggings and tunics and cloaks. Arma dried strips of meat, skewered on sharp sticks, over the fire they kept burning day and night. If they were to survive the winter, they must have food.

Now frost rimed the grass almost every morning, and it would not be many weeks before the snow came and covered the forest. Meat was necessary to keep them alive, with energy to move, if necessary.

Arma was strangely happy; she was busy, glad to be a part of a family once again. Bain, no longer a stranger, seemed closer than a brother and dearer than a friend. She had always felt nearer to Kalva than to her own kin, and she felt that this was a family of her own choosing. The Grandmother would have hissed at the thought.

Once she had the meat-drying in hand, she went about the task of making fish-hooks from the bones of hares, pounding the leg-bones into sharp splinters and tying them to finger-lengths of peeled twigs. Baited with chunks of fat or gut from the game and tied to cords made of sinew, they went into the deep water lower down the stream.

The first time she hauled in a big carp from the water, she was excited; she had supplied a need, all by herself. Kalva welcomed the change of diet, and Bain beamed at her as if she had done something wonderful.

She caught more, though not every day, and those they could not eat at once she sliced into strips and dried over her fires, along with rabbit and deer and woodchuck. They would need a lot of food, Bain warned her, for winters this far north were much harder than those in the grasslands. It would take a great deal of work to see them through the cold months when the snow was too deep for hunting.

In the evenings they sat before their fire, snug in the cave, and talked of all the things they needed to do in order to survive. The language they used was a mix of both tongues, and they had become so used to communicating in this way that they were able to agree without trouble.

They had to find a better place for the cold months. Kalva could not live through the winter exposed to the damp and cold that crept into this shallow space. Food and wood left outside its shelter would be covered with snow or stolen by wolves.

One chilly evening, Bain returned triumphantly from his day of hunting for game and new shelter. "I found a deep cave upstream," he said. "It isn't far, though it is not easy to see. We can move our things without too much trouble. We will need your baskets to carry the dried meat and the hides, but it won't take too long."

They had baskets, but they also needed nets, and Bain proved to be quick at learning how to weave them. He had done it as a child, for the women and children of the hunter people trapped birds and learned the craft early in their lives.

Arma wove several baskets so tightly that they would hold water, and Kalva smeared them inside with yellow clay from the riverbank. Then, building a tiny fire outside the cave on the apron of stone that was their doorstep, she propped her pots over it, one by one, turning them frequently as the clay hardened.

Several cracked and were unusable, but when they had one that did not, they had a pot in which they could boil their meat, along with herbs the women had gathered. Broth seemed to put new life into Kalva, whose snaggled teeth found meat hard to chew.

If Bain had found a home much farther away, they would have had a hard time moving the quantity of possessions they had accumulated with all their hard work. Even as it was, they had to make trip after trip to carry all the bags, bowls, weapons, and stores to the new cave.

Arma approved of the new location, for the entrance to the cave faced south, with water not too far below in the deep stream. Wood in abundance grew in the thick forest that leaned over the stream. Deadfall was easily found, and their complex of crooked tunnels and rounded rooms could be filled with dry wood to see them through the blizzards to come.

They saw no trace of other people. Even the hunters of Bain's tribe had not come so far east, he said, and the teeming game told them that no others came here, either. They kept hunting and drying meat, for there would be little game in the next months.

Though Arma's people had never known any people who lived under the ground, she found the cavern in which she now lived to be much less draughty and cold than even the best of the longhouses. Because a narrow crack in the roof carried away smoke, the air was not stifling, even when the fire was large.

They settled upon storerooms and sleeping places and the area for the permanent fire. Settling into a life that was not completely different from the one any of them knew, they found themselves far more comfortable than they would have thought, when they escaped with only the clothing on their backs.

Arma understood that each of them was condemned to death by his own people. That gave them a sense of mutual dependence and trust, which helped to knit them into a family. Even when disagreements arose, she knew too well how isolated they were; they could not risk quarreling.

Arma had never known a life so easy or so happy. There had always been the children to keep clean, to feed, to watch. Then she had been busy with Kalva, tending the sick and finding and preparing herbs. After that had come the threat of marriage, which had spoiled her pleasure in her work.

Now she sat before the fire with Bain and Kalva, sorting through the roots and leaves they had gathered and discussing possible uses with the healer. Bain made arrows and fletched them, stretched sinew for bowstring and cordage, and stayed as busy as the women did.

Sometimes Arma wondered if Bain was truly as contented as he seemed. She and Kalva needed his skills and his knowledge, in order to survive, but did he truly need the two of them? Had he suspected, months ago in the wood beside the village, how much his friendship with her might change his life?

More and more, though she said little about it, Arma found she did not believe in the things she had been taught about the Mother Goddess. That was sad, for in this dangerous world one needed gods to support the feeble efforts of a human being.

Bain talked often of the Horned God. His tale about his meeting with the great stag that sent him southward intrigued her. The Mother Goddess had never seemed a friend to her people, only a demanding presence and a threat, as the Grandmother showed her. A kind and helpful god was something she had not thought of before.

"I was so tired of whining children and sick villagers," she said one evening as they sat about their fire. "And the Grandmother seemed to grow more cruel all the time. I have no regrets, Kalva, about leaving our people."

Bain, busy weaving nets for fishing, looked at her across the stone ring that held the fire in place. "I wonder if your Grandmother will live for long, now that her people see that her goddess could not protect their people from attack. They must know what you and Kalva said to her, too."

He tied off a knot and bit the grass cord in two. "I have seen among my own people that when changes come the very old often die."

He began looping another area of his net. "In a year or two, you might go back to the village to see. They may need you badly by then."

The old woman nodded. "That is true. Elna is older than I, and she may not live out the winter. I might go back to see, if I survive. But not to live. I found the confusion of the village tiring, and I like being here alone with you two."

She smiled suddenly. "We might gather and prepare medicines and go back in summer to trade with them. That would give us a way to get well fired pots that we would find it hard to make for ourselves, or woven cloth, or even, perhaps, a pair of goats."

Arma braided a neat edge about the top of a basket and set it aside. She hugged her knees under her chin and stared into the fire. The thought excited her. If they waited long enough, surely it would be safe to return. Then they could trade furs, as well as medicines, for the things that would be difficult to make.

"We could live to ourselves," she said softly. "But we could go back, too. That would be a fine way to live!"

Bain nodded, his pale face and hair catching the red glow of the fire. "We might even have others want to join us. But not too many," he added hastily.

There came a great gust of wind that fluttered their fire, even so deep in the windings of the cave, and Bain sighed. "It will be a long time until spring. In my own village, even inside earth-covered lodges, the people will suffer from the cold. Some lose fingers and toes every winter, and often the old and the sick do not live until warm weather comes again.

"We are more comfortable here, with wood stored and food and plenty of skins, than they have ever been. We will talk and rest all winter, and tell tales, perhaps."

He tied off the end of his net and hung it from a boss of stone that thrust from the wall over his head. "What a strange year this has been!"

Arma took a rabbit skin from the pile that she intended to use to make into a cloak. "Why not make new tales, instead of telling only the old ones?" she asked. "We have wonderful things to make songs about, just the three of us. The battle we saw between our people is one. Rescuing Kalva. The wolf you killed. We have a great deal to sing about, Bain. We can make stories of our own."

"I never thought I would be a singer of tales," Bain said. "But why not? We all have done things we never did before, and if this is the beginning of a new clan we should make its story for those to come. We will not always be alone."

Arma knew that he was right. When she and Bain became mates, there would be children who must know the history of their people. They should begin at once to remember and to put into words all the things they knew from their tribes and from their own exciting escapes.

CHAPTER NINETEEN

THE BEAR

☼ARMA☼

The weather grew terrible. Icy winds were followed by deep snows that gave way to calm periods of brilliant sun and iron freezes. They did not leave the cavern at all for days at a time, and making songs of their adventures was a great comfort to all three.

Arma knew from the beginning that Kalva would be best at making new songs, for in her long life she had heard the great masters of their tribe, who were known for exciting and beautiful chants. But they all worked together, adding lines, disagreeing sometimes on details and yet feeling the thrill of achievement when they all sang the chant together.

Even then, time hung heavy, for at last there came an end even to necessary tasks. Even the songs became tiresome, in time, and they could only sleep for so many hours, waking, restless and irritable, at last.

Arma and Bain had a couple of fierce arguments

over nothing at all, but Kalva made them take a turn outside to cool off. "Winter is hard on everyone," the healer said. "We can't move outside, and there isn't enough room in the cave for a real walk. When we feel angry, let us go out onto the path leading up to the wood. That should make us appreciate our cave."

Indeed, a short while in the icy wind cooled the worst fit of temper quickly. Even the old woman had to take her own advice, from time to time, as the winter wore on.

It was a bitter season, with huge drifts of snow that all but clogged the mouth of the cave. The captives shared out their food stingily, knowing that it must last over the season. They ate once a day and spent much time wrapped in their warm furs, among which they numbered one with a most exciting story behind it.

That formed one of the best of their new songs, once the frantic activity was over. Early in the winter, before snow covered most of the cave's mouth, they were busy with their tasks. The fire had died to embers in the fire pit, and Kalva was deep in the cave, seeing to her strings of drying herbs.

Arma was in the tunnel in which they stored dried meat, getting out enough for their daily meal. Bain was sitting beside the pit, adding chunks of wood to make the fire roar.

Hearing his shout, Arma ran into the main chamber. Bain was sitting flat, staring up into the red eyes of a giant bear, whose sudden roar filled the cave, making bits of grit fall from the walls and roof. As Arma stood stunned, Bain leaped, though he could never afterward explain how, out of range of the bear's claws. When he landed, he was reaching into his kilt for his sling.

Kalva came dashing out of her herb room and stood, frozen, as the boy swung the sling. The first stone went wide, for Arma saw his hand shake. The second struck solidly between the scarlet eyes.

The bear was far from stunned. He charged, but luckily the roof was so low that he could not rise onto his hind legs. Bain flung another stone, which missed as the animal rushed forward into the fire pit with both front paws.

Its rumbling growl became a cry of pain; it stopped and sat down to lick its burned pads. Arma caught a spear from the wall behind her and handed it to Bain.

The boy ran forward and stabbed the fire-hardened point into the creature's side, just under its shoulder. Before it could rise, Arma was upon it with another spear; this thrust went deep into the neck.

Kalva, weaponless, sprang toward the bear, shrieking at the top of her shrill voice. Terrified and in pain, the beast rolled backward out of the tunnel and the cave-mouth. It rolled down the hill, gathering speed all the while, to fall into the river below the path.

Arma and Bain arrived in time to see the bear go into the cold black water. Bain sped down the track and was waiting when the huge head emerged, snorting, from its icy bath. Reaching out with his spear, the boy pushed the head under again, holding it down by wedging the haft of the spear under an overhanging rock.

The bear struggled, and the spear bobbed dangerously against the stone; Bain held it fast and the water was almost freezing. By that time the animal had lost a great deal of blood. The dark water grew even darker, as the bear drowned.

It took the three of them, using all their strength, to haul that huge carcass ashore. There they dressed it out by torchlight and cut the meat into chunks. The women carried those up in baskets, making trip after trip, while Bain dragged the heavy skin to safety.

Now that it was so cold they could keep the meat a long while without having to dry it, and there was enough flesh on the animal to last for many weeks. The thick layer of fat beneath the skin gave them tallow for lamps and for making greased bags that held water, as well.

Bain dressed the pelt and gave it to Kalva to warm her aching bones and cushion her from the hard floor beneath her grass pallet. He had already taken the time to dress the wolf skin properly, working in ashes, pounding and rubbing and working the skin until it was supple. No longer did it smell.

The bearskin, after the same sort of treatment, was beautiful to see, gleaming black and soft in the firelight. Kalva wrapped it about her as she worked and slept rolled in it at night, and Arma knew that it eased the pain of her stiff joints, for she moved more easily.

That was enough excitement for any winter, they agreed. No one craved more, and even in the worst of dull times they were grateful that they had no such problem to deal with. Working the adventure into a chant was far more comfortable.

Kalva finished first song, of course, and it was

the tale of Bain's killing the bear. They all learned it and chanted it together so often that it seemed always to have been a part of their store of tales.

Sitting about the fire, week after week, they fed fresh wood to the flames and sang their new songs, reliving dangers now safely in the past. It was good to remember hard times when you were warm and had a full belly.

But even then they dreamed of spring. Above them was a tremendous forest, strange to all of them, waiting to be explored when the weather cleared. New sorts of game would live there, new plants and trees and herbs with new uses.

There might be people, although Bain said he doubted that, for there was no story among his tribe of any men living in this direction. Yet there would be other things that would be fresh and new and interesting to examine and explore.

They watched the mountains across the river, when they could see them on clear days when the blizzards rested. Arma dreamed of a summer spent differently from any that she remembered. She thought they all would find this next year the best of all their lives.

CHAPTER TWENTY

THE HORNED ONE

 **BAIN**

Bain had decided that winter would last forever, leaving them frozen and dried to bones in the cave, when the weather broke at last. They had made more baskets and nets and clothing than a dozen people could use, working to keep from going crazy with boredom.

Kalva had found clay in the depths of the cave and made pots and bowls and dishes, firing them at the edge of the fire pit. Yet even she had given up at last, amid stacks of pottery that would hold seeds and herbs found the next summer.

Stories wore thin and even their songs palled. They all were frantic to be out and doing, long before the sun began to melt the deep drifts of snow.

But in time the winds shifted and the sun shone for hours every day. The ice on the river began to thin and then to break, and Bain heard grindings in the night that told him the current beneath was shifting the cakes of ice. And then the snows melted in earnest, making the river run bank-full.

It was as well that their cave was high up in the wall of the stream, or else they might have been flooded out. As soon as they could manage, Bain and Arma wrapped themselves in furs and stepped out onto the doorstone, which had been buried for so long in snow and ice.

The sun was very bright, sparkling on the icicles hanging from the trees over the river and from the ice that coated the stones below. From time to time there came a musical tinkle as ice dropped from trees in the wood above.

They climbed to the top of the cliff and looked about at the forest. Snow still covered the ground in spots, but a few hardy shoots of green already were pushing up through the wet mulch.

Arma ran to gather a patch of pale leaves. "This will give our stew some flavor tonight!" she yelled.

They went back quickly, for it was still very cold, but the next day Kalva ventured to go with them. She and Arma went into the wood and returned with even more fresh sprouts. Bain found that with the addition of the greenery the sore spots inside his mouth disappeared quickly.

The boy was happy. Sometimes he felt guilty, knowing that a year before his father had been alive and was now dead, but he couldn't help it. He was more comfortable than he had ever been among his own people. Even his longing to see his mother and sisters had dwindled, through the cold months.

Kalva was wise, that was part of it. She knew as much, at least, as the Shaman, and with it she was kind. Arma was like one of his own sisters, but with an intriguing difference that he was just beginning to feel strongly. In time the three of them would be a real family, he knew.

But this would be a different kind of family. In the tribe, mates were chosen by their parents or the Shaman. This time he had chosen for himself, and Arma had, as well. He found such freedom intoxicating.

* * * * * * *

His tiny clan did not stay inside once the weather turned warmer. They stopped off the storage tunnels so that wandering beasts would not rummage through their supplies, and they hung their extra weapons, nets, and other equipment high so that nothing could reach and destroy them.

Taking only what they needed, they went out to spend time camping in the forest. By day they went in three different directions, pursuing their own interests, but at night they returned to camp. Bain soon taught the women the secrets of remaining alive in the forest, and so quick were they that he did not worry as much as he might have when they were on their own.

Though he was still concerned about them, even as he tracked game or watched the squirrels mating high in the beeches, after all his concern he was the one who came to grief.

Returning to camp one evening, carrying three hares over his shoulder, he was fingering a bright pebble he had put into his pouch. It was fully the match for the one he had given Arma, and he felt that finding it had been a good omen. He felt particularly strong and fit as he moved surely down the stony path.

Something shifted beneath him as a rocky shelf split away from the rest of the hillside. The world dropped from beneath him, and he tumbled into a hollow space tunneled out by an underground stream. Striking a stone, he felt the bone in his leg snap, filling him with sick despair.

He lay on his back, staring up at the circle of sky above, which was now dark blue and held a single star. When he tried moving, he found that he was wedged in among flat plates of shale, which shifted beneath him.

The motion wrenched his leg, and agony shot through him, bringing tears to his eyes. The movement set other layers of shale in motion, and another small ledge slipped down on top of him. He found that he couldn't push it away.

How strange, Bain thought, to run so far, to escape such dangers, and then to come to his death in such a silly way. Here in this alien place, far from kinfolk or even his new family, he had found his end.

Death came, of course, to everyone and was nothing to worry about. Not one of his people dreaded that time. He could only wait patiently for the sky to darken and his breath to still.

He wondered now about the Horned One. Had the great stag sent him southward to find his death? Was this his punishment for defying the Shaman? But no, he could not feel that to be true. There had been only good will in those soft dark eyes into which had looked, there in the forest so long ago.

The sky grew darker. Kalva had taught her charges a long call to use in case of need. He raised his head as much as possible and shouted into the dimness, but his voice echoed around and around the well of stone. Only the call of an owl came in answer.

He leaned back, relaxing as much as possible. The air was growing chilly; he would have liked to die with his wolf skin about him. But he turned his thoughts away. One who had killed both a wolf and a bear needed nothing to make his dying easy.

He thought of the Shaman. Was he alive? Did he still curse him for flouting his will? He had done what was right, he had no doubt, no matter what the ancient might think. Perhaps it was his curse that had brought this upon him.

He dozed, but a terrible pain in his leg woke him. He called again, just for something to do, and this time he heard an answer, very faint and far away.

Again Bain pushed himself up as far as possible. "Coooooooeeeeeeee!" he yelled, taking most of his strength with the cry.

The owl said something irritable from the tree above, but along with that came a human voice. Arma. He would know her voice anywhere.

How had she tracked him, and why had she known that he needed help? He had covered many miles as he hunted, and he was not returning along his original track. How could she possibly know? How could she have found him?

There was a pale glow on the rim of stone above him, and he knew the full moon was rising. That would provide light, when she came. It would take work to get him out of here. Hauling up that bear had not been much worse, he was sure.

The moon's disc edged into view, and the voice was nearer. Bain stared up at the moon as it rose over the edge of the hole. In that round eye of light there was a pair of antlers...huge, branching antlers.

A stag stared down into the darkness as if it looked into his eyes. Was it the Horned One?

He knew that it must be. The great head turned, the horns catching glints of light from the moon. He stared up at the creature, feeling its gaze strike deep into his heart.

The Shaman was wrong. The Horned God was wild and fierce and free, but he was not cruel and capricious. He did not punish people who did not obey him, Bain was certain, as the silhouetted head bent over him. He felt no anger there, only a sort of curious concern.

Feet grated on stone. Behind and above, he could hear Arma and Kalva moving toward him, picking their way carefully down the slant of the shale. A hand touched his shoulder, and gravels slid down behind his head.

Kalva's awed whisper came from behind him. "That is a sign, Bain. The Great One led us to you, all the way from our camp. He bugled among the trees until we came, and then he led us, moving slowly so we could keep him in sight."

Now Arma's hand touched his shoulder and he could see her face as she looked up to regard the Horned One.

"He will be the god of our clan," she said, her tone unafraid. "We will not make sacrifices to him, for he does not want that. The Mother Goddess is far behind in the farmlands, and here we are in the keeping of the Horned God. He will be the protector of our family."

"We are the children of the Horned One," Bain murmured, feeling himself slipping into darkness.

"Yes," said Kalva.

Now the moon's disc was full and round, standing on edge on the rim above. The great head moved and was gone as if it had never been.

Bain stirred, and the women began digging cautiously to free him. It would take a long while, and it would be painful, but they would get him out, in time. Borne up by the wonder of the thing they had seen, they would carry him to camp in triumph.

Even as he fainted at last, Bain understood. They would thrive, here in the great forest. He and Arma would have many children, and Kalva would live to great old age, teaching and guiding them all. And the Horned One would be there, his rack of antlers held high, his soft eyes watching over his chosen clan.

All would be well with his people.

www.ingramcontent.com/pod-product-compliance
Lightning Source LLC
Chambersburg PA
CBHW020653180626
46816CB00003B/1268